For a wench known as Lisa.

The Day It Rained Diamonds

KENDELL FOSTER CROSSEN
Writing as
M.E. CHABER

STEEGER BOOKS / **2020**

PUBLISHED BY STEEGER BOOKS
Visit steegerbooks.com for more books like this.

PUBLISHING HISTORY

Hardcover
New York: Holt, Rinehart & Winston (A Rinehart Suspense Novel), October 1966.
Toronto: Holt, Rinehart & Winston of Canada, 1966.
London: MacDonald & Co. (A Boardman Mystery), 1968.

Paperback
New York: Paperback Library (63-231), A Milo March Mystery, #3, January 1970. Cover by Robert McGinnis.

ISBN: 978-1-61827-536-3

Milo March is a hard-drinking, womanizing, wisecracking, James-Bondian character. He always comes out on top through a combination of personality, bluff, bravado, luck, skill, experience, and intellect. He is a shrewd judge of human character, a crack shot, and a deeper character than I have found in most of the other spy/thriller novels I've read. But, above all, he is a con-man—and a very good one. It is Milo March himself who makes the series worth reading.

—Don Miller, *The Mystery Nook* fanzine 12

Steeger Books is proud to reissue twenty-three vintage novels and stories by M.E. Chaber, whose Milo March Mysteries deliver mile-a-minute action and breezily readable entertainment for thriller buffs.

Milo is an Insurance Investigator who takes on the tough cases. Organized crime, grand theft, arson, suspicious disappearances, murders, and millions and millions of dollars—whatever it is, Milo is just the man for the job. Or even the only man for it.

During World War II, Milo was assigned to the OSS and later the CIA. Now in the Army Reserves, with the rank of Major, he is recalled for special jobs behind the Iron Curtain. As an agent, he chops necks, trusses men like chickens to steal their uniforms, shoots point blank at secret police—yet shows compassion to an agent from the other side.

Whatever Milo does, he knows how to do it right. When the work is completed, he returns to his favorite things: women, booze, and good food, more or less in that order....

THE MILO MARCH MYSTERIES

CONTENTS

ONE

It was supposed to be a vacation, the first one I'd had in a couple of years. A friend of mine was a director out in Hollywood, which meant that he lived in Beverly Hills and worked in Universal City, Burbank, Rome, or London. Anyway, he was going to Europe for a few weeks and suggested that I use his pad for my vacation. It sounded great when I heard about it in New York. He was a bachelor and offered to throw in his little black book—which made it sound even greater. I accepted his offer and caught the next plane to California.

Me? I'm Milo March, insurance investigator. At least, that's what it says on the door of my office on Madison Avenue in New York City. And enough insurance companies believe it to keep me working most of the time. That's why I needed a vacation.

I arrived at the International Airport in Los Angeles in time to meet my friend and get the key to his place before he took a plane for New York and then Rome. I wished him luck and he wished me luck, and then we were on our own. I had arranged to rent a car, which was waiting, a nice, shining white Cadillac convertible. I signed for it and headed east.

My friend had an apartment up above the Strip, barely within the city limits of Beverly Hills. I drove up to it and parked in front of the garage.

It was a nice pad—two bedrooms, living room, dining room, and kitchen, all furnished in modern Chinese. And it included a window with a good view of the swimming pool, which I immediately saw was crowded with shapely girls in scanty bathing suits. A perfect vacation spot.

I checked the larder. There was food in the freezer and there was plenty of booze. I made myself a dry martini and sat down to contemplate my vacation. It was a nice thought. After the second martini, I decided to do something about it. I picked up the black book and started looking through it. My friend had marked a few pages with slips of paper on which he had scrawled brief descriptions.

The first one was Lita Harper. The slip of paper stated that she was attractive, intelligent, and witty, and was good company. It sounded like just what I needed for my first evening in California. I picked up the phone and dialed her number.

"Johnny?" she asked when she picked up the phone. It was an interesting voice.

"I'm afraid not," I said. "My name is Milo March. Jed Moore is a friend of mine and loaned me his apartment while I'm here for a rest. He suggested that I might enjoy meeting you, so I'm phoning to ask if you'll have dinner with me tonight."

"Oh," she said. At first, she sounded disappointed, but then her voice picked up as she went on in a rush of words. "How is dear Jed? I haven't seen him in months."

"He's fine. Or was this afternoon when I saw him off for Rome."

She laughed. "Oh, yes. Jed is fond of those wild Italian girls. Have you known him long?"

"Years and years. Suppose we discuss him over dinner tonight?"

"All right," she said. "Pick me up at eight. If Jed gave you my phone number, he probably also gave you my address?"

"He did."

She laughed. "Some friend. All right, I'll see you at eight." She hung up.

I unpacked my things, then shaved and took a long shower. I put on a robe and went back to the living room. It had a large window from which I could see most of Los Angeles. At least, I could if the smog didn't get too heavy.

The shower had cut down my mileage on the martini, so I made another. It was still several hours before my date. I turned on the television and listened to an early newscast, feeling pretty smug about the fact that none of the news could have anything to do with me for at least two weeks. I watched and sipped my martini. When I'd finished it, I turned off the television and stretched out on the bed for a short nap. I was still three hours ahead of California time.

I awakened an hour later, which was the way I had planned it. I splashed cold water on my face, got dressed, and took a fond look at my gun and holster, thankful that I didn't have to wear them. It was time to go. I went out and got into the Cadillac.

Lita Harper's apartment was not far away from my borrowed place. I drove slowly, enjoying every minute of having nothing to do except enjoy myself. She lived in another of those large apartment buildings, perched on the side of a hill and looking as if it were about to topple over.

I pressed the button under her name and then went upstairs to the second floor when the buzzer sounded.

She opened the door just before I reached it. The sight was more than I had expected. She was a doll. About five feet eight, with curves in all the proper places, topped off with a beautiful face and shining black hair down to her shoulders.

"Hello, Milo," she said.

"Hello, Lita," I answered. "How did you know I was the right one?"

"It's eight o'clock," she said. "That's the time you were supposed to be here. Come in while I get my wrap."

I stepped into an apartment that was so beautiful and luxurious that I was afraid to breathe; I might have left a spot of alcohol on something. Fortunately, she was back before I began to turn purple in the face.

We went downstairs and out to the car. I helped her into it and went around to slide under the wheel.

"Where are we going?" she asked.

"It's your town, honey," I said. "I'm a stranger. Pick what you like and that's where we go."

"All right, but don't complain when you get the check. Just follow my directions."

"Okay. You really live in that apartment?"

"Of course. Why?"

"I was afraid to move while I was in there for fear I'd leave a spot on something."

She laughed. "I guess Jed didn't tell you what I do?"

"No gossip," I said.

"I am an interior decorator. I live in the apartment, but it is also my showplace. I decorated Jed's apartment. Do you like it?"

"Yes, but I must confess I found myself getting slightly nervous there. You should see my place in New York."

"What period is it? Modern?"

"Shiftless American."

She laughed again, and I decided that I liked the sound.

I followed her directions and we finally ended up at a restaurant just south of Sunset. It was elegant enough to make me feel certain that the food would be good. She was recognized, and we were led to a good table in the corner of the room.

I had a martini and she had a manhattan, and we began to get acquainted. The process involved several cocktails and most of the dinner, which was as excellent as I'd expected. By that time we had a warm relationship, and I was finding it a pleasant evening.

After dinner we hit a couple of night spots. Then she suggested that we go, even though it was not late as time goes in such places.

"You'll have to tell me how to get back to your place," I told her as we got into the car. "By this time, I'm lost."

"You don't even know how to get back to Jed's apartment," she said, "so I'd better tell you how to get there first. Besides, I'd like to see how Jed is treating my creations."

I was raised never to argue with a lady, so I followed her instructions until we arrived in front of Jed's apartment building. We went inside, and I flicked on the lights. She stopped just inside the doorway, looking at the living room. I thought her artistic feelings might be upset by the martini glass I'd left on the coffee table, but she ignored it.

"It looks just the same," she said with satisfaction. "This was one of my least expensive jobs, but I must admit that it has always pleased me."

"Sit down and drink it in," I suggested, "while I get you something more liquid to drink." On my way to the kitchen I scooped up the martini glass and took it along.

We'd been drinking bourbon on the rocks, so that was what I fixed for us. I carried the drinks into the living room. She was sitting on the couch, obviously still enjoying her own work. I handed her the drink.

"Lovely," she said.

"Thank you," I said modestly. "It's really nothing. All you do is put some ice cubes in a glass, then cover them with bourbon, preferably a good brand."

She looked at me and smiled. "I didn't mean to talk about the apartment. But you are comfortable in it, aren't you, Milo?"

I nodded. "I like it—but to tell you the truth I'd hate to live here all the time."

"Why?"

"I'd probably have a nervous breakdown. I'd always be afraid that I was going to spill ashes or a drink somewhere, and before I could clean it up, the decorator would suddenly drop in for a look at her masterpiece. One look at what I had done and she would be gone—never to return again. Despondent, I would commit *hari-kari*—whatever it is the Japanese do—on the rug, thereby ruining it beyond repair."

She laughed. "All right, Milo. No more talk about my work. And if you drop ashes on Jed's rug, I'll try to ignore it. I just realized that we have spent most of the evening talking about Jed or me. It's hardly the way to treat a visitor. Tell me about Milo March. I promise you my full attention."

"You won't need that much," I told her. "I work in insurance. I'm single. I live in a three-room apartment in Greenwich Village. It was furnished and decorated, I imagine, by the little secondhand store around the corner. I have an office on Madison Avenue. I like women, booze, and food, more or less in that order. There you are, a complete autobiography."

"There must be more to it than that. What do you do in insurance? Sell it?"

"Heaven forbid. I'm a specialist. I run errands for a vice-president."

"That doesn't sound very exciting."

"It is when I get paid. Remember the three things I told you I liked? They're a lot of fun, but they're all expensive."

As we continued to talk, I began to revise some of my earlier impressions of her. For one thing, I had been surprised when she'd suggested coming to the apartment with me. My first evaluation of that had been the obvious one. I was changing my mind about it. She didn't act like a woman who was prepared for fun and games.

For one thing, while she was still a charming and entertaining talker, her mind wasn't with it. She was thinking of something else. And she kept taking fast glances at her watch as though she were on a tight schedule. I've been around enough not to have my masculine pride unduly disturbed, but it did make me curious.

She took another peek at her watch, then suddenly leaned over and put out her half-smoked cigarette. I knew that she was about to announce a decision.

"I have to go, Milo," she said. "Thank you for a lovely evening."

"What's your hurry? Do you turn into a pumpkin at a certain hour?"

This time there was a hint of nervousness in her laughter. "Nothing so mundane. I'm sorry, Milo. I don't suppose it's a very nice thing to do, but I—I have to go see someone."

"A little late for interior decorating, isn't it?"

"This is personal. I will see you again—if you want me to."

"Of course I do," I said. "All right, come on. I'll drive you wherever you want to go."

We were both standing up by this time, and she had recovered her wrap from the couch.

"No, that won't be necessary," she said. Her white teeth gnawed briefly at her lower lip. "As a matter of fact, I'm seeing someone who lives in this building. I don't know how long I'll be, so I'll take a taxi when I leave." She put her hand on my arm. "Milo, you're a dear. Please call me soon. I promise that nothing will interfere with our next date."

"Sure," I said.

I held the door open for her and resisted the temptation to watch and see where she went. After I'd gone back into the apartment, I took off my coat and hung it up and undid my tie. Then I made myself a big drink and sat on the couch. The lingering scent of her perfume was still in the air.

"Milo, you're a dear," I said to myself. "You're also a jerk." I sat down on the couch, took a drink, and stared out at the Christmas-tree view of Los Angeles at night.

Well, I had the answer to one thing. I knew why she had suggested coming back to the apartment with me. That was where she had her late date. But it seemed to be the only answer I did have.

I pondered the possibilities. It was only midnight, but it was probably too late to call any of the other numbers in Jed's book. I could go out and do a little pub crawling, but there wouldn't be too much time for that because I knew the bars had to close at two in the morning. Finally, I laughed and decided to be philosophical about the whole thing. I turned on the television set and switched to the Johnny Carson show.

Stretching out, with my feet hanging over the other side of the coffee table ("No shoes on the Mandarin table, my fine interior decorator!"), I relaxed and began enjoying the show and the bourbon. I was glad that I hadn't gone out, for I suddenly realized that I was tired. The three hours' difference in time between New York and Los Angeles was catching up with me.

The Carson show finished, I turned on a late movie and made myself another drink, intending to finish it and then go to bed no matter what was happening on the small screen.

I was slipping into that happy euphoric state which comes just before you get up and stumble off to bed. Cary Grant was still carrying on with a pretty broad on the screen. I was watching it, but my eyes were becoming glazed.

Then there was a sound like two quick gunshots. My eyes went to the screen even though I knew that Cary Grant wouldn't shoot the good-looking broad. No, he was kissing her. At that point I came fully awake and sat up. Reason returned and I felt foolish. No one was going to be shooting anyone in a nice, expensive place like this. It must have been a car backfiring. I relaxed again and reached for my drink.

Then a woman screamed. It was so close that I spilled part of the drink on my shirt. I checked the screen again. No, the broad wasn't screaming; she seemed to be enjoying what was happening.

The screaming continued. I got up and walked over to the door, opening it far enough to listen for a minute. There was no question but that the screams were coming from within the building. It sounded like somewhere on the floor above. I hesitated only a minute. There was always the chance of barging into a husband-wife fight and having both of them jump you. But this didn't sound like that sort of screaming. I went back inside, got my gun, checked it to be sure it was loaded, then went out and hurried up the stairs.

I wasn't the only one. There were five people standing in the hallway—three men and two women, all of them wearing robes over pajamas or nightgowns. They were clustered against the wall across from a closed door. There was no doubt that the screaming was coming from that apartment, although now it sounded more like a wail.

One of the men looked at me, his gaze shifting from my face to the gun in my hand. "Are you a policeman?" he asked uncertainly.

"No," I said. "I'm staying downstairs. What's going on?"

"We don't know," one of the women said. "We heard two shots and she started screaming."

"I called the police right away," the man said. "They should be here by now." He was still looking uncertainly at my gun.

"Did anybody knock on the door or try to open it?" I asked.

They all stared at each other, then turned to look at me, shaking their heads. I walked across the hallway and knocked on the door. The screaming stopped only to be replaced by hysterical sobbing, which was almost as loud. There was no other sound from within the apartment. I knocked again, but nothing happened.

"I called the police," the man said again. "They'll be here soon. They are very prompt in Beverly Hills."

"Sure," I said, "the cops will be here, but in the meantime someone may be getting killed in there."

Having taken a position, I was faced with a problem. If I tried the door, I might ruin important fingerprints. If I merely broke in the door and there was nothing seriously wrong, I might find myself charged with breaking and entering. In the meantime, the woman inside was still sobbing, breathing with a sound that was just short of a scream.

Fortunately I was saved from making a decision. There was the wail of a siren moaning to a stop in front of the building. A moment later there was the buzz of several bells and the sound of pounding on the building front door.

"Oh," one of the women said. She darted into the apartment right back of her and then the front door buzzer sounded.

Two cops came along with drawn guns, looking around.

"Right up here, officers," one of the men said.

The two cops came up the stairs. "What's going on here?" one of them asked.

"We're not sure, officer," the same man said. "We heard what sounded like two shots and then a woman started screaming. Now she is only sobbing. I am the one who called you."

"And then this man," one of the women said, pointing at me, "came running up the stairs waving a gun."

For the first time the two cops looked at me. One of them pointed his gun at me.

"All right," he said, "take it easy. Just reverse that gun slowly and hand it to me."

I did as he said.

"Now," he continued, "who'd you shoot?"

"Nobody," I said in disgust. "I'm staying downstairs in the apartment of a friend. I heard the same things the others did and came upstairs."

"Fine," the cop said. "Just don't go anywhere. All of you get over on this side of the wall. If there's any shooting, you'll be safer there."

The five people scurried across the hallway. I partially joined them, but managed to stay far enough out so I could see into the apartment when they got the door opened.

One of the cops knocked on the door. There was no answer. He knocked again. "Police," he said. "Open up." This didn't buy him anything either. He looked at his partner.

"Try the door," the second cop said.

"Oh, yeah," the first one said. He reached down and tried the doorknob. The door swung open.

The two cops looked inside and forgot about the rest of us. They almost knocked each other over getting inside.

"Get on the phone and call Homicide," one of them snapped. "Give them the address and tell them we'll leave everything as it is."

They certainly weren't paying any attention to us, so I moved around to where I could look into the room.

There was a man stretched out on the floor. The front of his shirt was almost completely red, and from the position of his body I was certain he wasn't alive. But that wasn't what caught my attention.

There was a woman crouched on the floor beside him, her face distorted and streaked with tears. There was a gun in her right hand. It was Lita Harper.

TWO

While it was not exactly what I'd expected to see, I can't say that I was completely surprised once I recognized her. I stepped into the room. After all, the cop had told me to stick around.

"Please, lady," one cop was saying while the other was busy on the phone. "Just give me the gun. Nice and easy like."

I don't think she heard him or even knew that he reached down and gingerly took the gun from her hand. Once she looked up, staring straight at me but with no sign of recognition. Then her head went down and she continued sobbing.

The older cop replaced the phone and turned around. "They'll be right here. In the meantime, don't touch anything."

"I had to take the gun away from her," the younger cop protested. "I couldn't just let her sit there waving it around."

"Yeah, but put it down before you mess up the fingerprints." He caught sight of me. "What are you doing here?"

"You told me to stick around."

"Oh, you're the guy with the gun. Well, stay put." He looked at the doorway where the other people were now clustered, enjoying every gory detail. "The rest of you people go back to your apartments."

"That woman," one of the women said, pointing at Lita, "came here a lot. I saw her in the hallway almost every day."

"That's fine, lady," the cop answered. "Just go back to your apartment and somebody will be there to talk to you about it." The five people withdrew reluctantly.

While we were waiting, the older cop came over to me, taking out his notebook and pencil. "What's your name?" he asked.

"Milo March."

"You say you live in this building?"

"No. I said I was staying in this building. Apartment one, downstairs. It is leased by a friend of mine, Jed Moore. I just came out here on my vacation, and since he was going to Europe he offered to let me use his apartment."

"On vacation from where?"

"New York City."

"You always carry a gun when you go on your vacation?"

"Nearly always."

He sighed heavily and put away the notebook. "All right. Stay put."

It was only a few more minutes before the building buzzer sounded, and the cop walked over to press the button to open the front door. A moment later a bunch of men trooped into the apartment. One man had a camera and began setting up his equipment. Another was obviously the medical examiner. There was a third man also carrying a bag, and I guessed he was the fingerprint man. When he opened his case, I saw that I had guessed right. Then there were two plainclothes detectives and a policewoman. At a nod from one of the detectives she went over, helped Lita off the floor, and led her to the couch.

The detective looked around and spotted the gun on the floor where the cop had placed it.

"Is that where the gun was?"

"No, sir," the younger cop said. He nodded toward Lita. "She was holding it."

"You handled it?"

"No, sir. Just the tip of the barrel as I took it away from her."

"Okay. Tell me what happened when you answered the call."

"Well, we got here and somebody pushed a button to let us in. There were six people standing out there in the hallway, including this guy who had a gun in his hand. We took his gun and then Frank knocked on the door. The only sound was the woman crying in here. Finally, Frank tried the door and it wasn't locked. When we came in we saw about the same thing you did. The guy was stretched out on the floor and the woman was squatted down beside him, crying and holding the gun. Frank took it away from her and I phoned in."

"Where are the other people?"

"I sent them back to their apartments and told them we'd be around to get their stories."

The detective nodded. He walked over and looked down at the dead man. "Know who he is?" he asked.

"Only what it says downstairs," the uniformed man said. "Renaldi is the name there."

"Yeah. Johnny Renaldi. A record as long as your arm. Who's the woman?"

"Don't know, sir. She hasn't said a word since we entered."

"Her name's Lita Harper," I said.

The detective glanced at me. "You know her?"

"Not exactly. We have a mutual friend, and I took her to dinner tonight. She came back here with me and had a drink downstairs. Then she left, saying that she was seeing someone in this building."

"Did she say who?"

"No."

"When did she leave your apartment?"

"About two hours ago."

He looked at the older cop. "This fellow got a name?"

"Yes, sir." The cop pulled out his notebook. "Says his name is Milo March and he's staying downstairs. Apartment one."

"All right," the detective said. "Have your partner leave this fellow's gun here and then you can go back to your cruiser. Marty, you go talk to the other tenants." The second detective nodded and left, soon followed by the uniformed officers. The detective turned back to me.

"What's your name?" he asked.

"The same as the officer told you. Milo March."

"You live here?"

"No, that is not what I told the officer. A friend of mine, Jed Moore, leases the apartment. I came out here on my vacation, and since my friend was leaving for Rome he offered me the use of his apartment. I accepted."

"He's in Rome now?"

"He left this afternoon … or, rather, yesterday afternoon. I saw him at the airport when I was arriving and he was leaving."

"I don't suppose it'll be easy to reach him in order to check your story?"

"Not immediately, but he will be sending me his address. In the meantime, you can check with the manager of the building. My friend told him that I would be staying in the apartment."

"All right," he said. "Tell me what happened tonight from your point of view."

"I was about ready to go to bed," I said. "I was having a drink and watching an old Cary Grant movie on television. I heard what I first thought were two gunshots. Then I decided I must be wrong. I started to relax again when the screaming started."

"Did you know who was screaming?" he interrupted.

"How the hell can you recognize a scream?"

"All right. Go ahead."

"I opened the apartment door and could tell that the screaming was coming from this floor, so I came up to see if I could do anything."

"Carrying your gun?" he asked gently.

"That's right."

"Why?"

I smiled at him. "I'd also heard two shots, remember. I've never discovered a way to catch bullets in my teeth. If someone is going to shoot at me, I want to be able to shoot back."

"Do you always carry a gun on your vacation?"

"I don't always carry a gun, but I usually take one with me."

"Why?"

"The reasons already mentioned above."

"You say you're on vacation, Mr. March. Where is your home?"

"New York City."

"I imagine from your attitude that you have a New York gun permit?"

"Yes."

"You're aware that such a permit is of no value here?"

"Yes."

He closed his eyes as though he were very tired. "All right, I'll ask the leading question. Do you have a gun permit that is good here?"

"I do."

"May I see it, please?"

I took my wallet and opened it to the California permit. I handed the open wallet to him.

He studied it for a minute. "Very interesting," he said. "What business are you in, Mr. March, that requires having a gun?"

"I'm an insurance investigator."

"An insurance investigator? I suppose you have a private detective's license?"

"Yes."

"In New York?"

"Yes."

"And do you have a California license?" he asked hopefully.

"I do."

He sighed again. "But no California office?"

"As a matter of fact, I do. It's in the Intercontinental Insurance Company's offices on Wilshire Boulevard."

"Do you have your California license with you?"

"Yes. It's on the other side of the permit."

He flipped it over and looked at it. "Sometimes," he said, "I think they pass a lot of laws just to make it tougher for cops. How long are you going to be here, March?"

"I expect to be here for three or four weeks."

"At this address?"

"Yes."

"If not, I can find you through Intercontinental Insurance?"

"Yes."

"I suppose you just happen to have something that shows you work for them?"

I smiled at him. "Flip two more cards and you'll see it."

He looked and handed my wallet back to me. "It's late," he said. "I'll let you go if you'll come in tomorrow and make a statement."

"Sure. What time?"

He glanced at his watch. "Better make it in the afternoon. Now beat it. I've got work to do."

"What about my gun?"

"It'll have to be checked out. If it's clean, you can pick it up tomorrow when you come in to make the statement."

"Who do I ask for?"

"Lieutenant Nathan O'Brien."

"All right, Lieutenant," I said with a smile. "Take good care of her. I may want to see her when I come in tomorrow."

He gave me a sour look. "You've been reading too many cheap novels. Get out."

"Thank you, Lieutenant," I said gently. "What do I do if someone tries to shoot me while you have my gun?"

"Call the police," he snapped.

"You know," I said in mock surprise, "I never thought of that. Good night, Lieutenant."

I left the apartment and went downstairs. The Cary Grant picture was over, but there was another picture on. I locked the door and took off my clothes. I had been sleepy before, but now I was wide awake. I made myself a big drink and watched the movie for a couple of minutes, then decided it wasn't for me. I turned the set off, lit a cigarette, and picked up my drink. I stared out the window at Los Angeles. The view was just as bright and just about as exciting as what had been on the TV screen.

Something was bothering me. It was true that I didn't know Lita Harper very well, but I had spent about four hours with her and she hadn't acted like someone who was going out to gun down a man—even a lover. Hysterics, yes. She had already demonstrated the possibility of that. Yet murder didn't seem to fit.

On the other hand, she had been crouched over the corpse with a gun in her hand—and only two or three minutes after the sound of the shots. She would have to have a damned good explanation. She would need a better one if the gun she was holding had killed a man and her prints were the only ones on it. Any way you looked at it, she was in for a tough time.

The Lieutenant had mentioned that the dead man had a long record. That puzzled me, too. Lita Harper hadn't looked like the sort of woman who would go for a hood, but then you could never tell. I'd known some very nice broads who fell for creeps. You can never tell how the ball is going to bounce when there's a broad pitching.

The drink relaxed me, so I finally put my cigarette out and went to bed. I couldn't find any answers just sitting there, and I was suddenly very tired. I was barely in bed before I was asleep.

The phone woke me up. Instead of ringing, it had one of those damned chimes, which is more penetrating than any ring. I pried my eyes open and looked at my watch. It was only eight o'clock—which meant I'd had almost four hours of sleep. I thought of just taking the phone off the hook and forgetting about it, but I knew I'd only worry about the call, so I propped myself up on one elbow and reached for the phone.

"Hello," I said with an effort.

"Mr. Milo March?" the operator asked.

"Speaking," I said, although I wasn't sure that was an accurate description of what I was doing.

"New York is calling. Your party is on the line, sir."

"Hello, Milo," another voice said.

I groaned at the sound. It was Martin Raymond, vice-president of Intercontinental Insurance.

"Martin," I said patiently, "why are you calling at such an ungodly hour?"

"What do you mean, Milo? It's eleven o'clock."

"Not out here, sweetheart. It's eight o'clock in the morning. Repeat, in the morning."

"What's wrong with that? I was up at seven this morning."

"You're a working stiff. I am on what we laughingly call a vacation. Under such circumstances eight o'clock is like bedtime."

"Oh, that's right, you're on vacation," he said jovially. "How's it going, boy?"

"I don't know," I said sourly. "It only started yesterday and I spent most of that traveling. And you call me at eight o'clock in the morning just to see if I'm having a happy vacation. Is that it?"

"Not exactly," he admitted. "Milo, I have a job for you."

"I'm on vacation," I protested.

"I know," he said soothingly, "but this is an important case. If you can handle it, we'll give you a generous bonus in addition to your daily rate—and expenses." The last two words were wrung from him as though he were giving up a lung.

"So you want me to run up to your office on Madison Avenue. It's too long a run, Martin. Besides, when *you're* on vacation, I don't call to tell you I need a job. So let's forget it."

"Milo, the job is out there. You don't have to go anywhere."

"Out here?"

"Yes. Have you seen the morning paper?"

"How the hell could I?" I asked. "You just got me out of a sound sleep."

"Well, both parts of it are in the papers here this morning, so they must have picked it up out there. This Harper woman—"

"Who?" I interrupted.

"A Lita Harper. We carry an insurance policy on her with a notice clause on any cancellation. She is now charged with murder, and if she's convicted, she may be executed before we can cancel."

I reached over and got a cigarette and lit it. "How big a policy?" I asked.

"Half a million."

"A good round number," I said. "What do you want me to do?"

"Check it out. If she's not guilty, prove it. If she is, I guess all we can do is try to stall until we can cancel."

"You're all heart, Martin," I said.

"Don't give me any sermons," he snapped.

I knew by the tone of his voice that more was involved than a mere life insurance policy—even one for half a million.

"Tell me the rest of the story," I said wearily.

"How did you know there was more?"

"There has to be. You forget how long I've known you, Martin."

"There's more," he said grimly. "For months there has been a series of jewel robberies out there—mostly in Beverly Hills. I believe that the total is now around three million dollars, but I know that we are involved for two million dollars. None of the jewelry has shown up and no one has been arrested for the thefts. That's a lot of money."

"I've heard," I said dryly. "Do you mean that you think Lita Harper had something to do with the baubles?"

"I don't know, Milo. But I do know that the only suspect the Beverly Hills police had was a criminal named Johnny Renaldi. He is the man who was murdered last night, and Lita Harper is charged with his murder."

"Sounds like an interesting situation," I observed. "But you forget that I'm on vacation."

"To hell with your vacation," he yelled. "This is a serious situation. And you're on the spot."

"Send me two thousand by Western Union. I'll go to work as soon as I receive it."

There was a moment of silence. "All right. Where do I send it?"

I gave him the address. "How'd you get my phone number?"

"Your answering service. I told them it was a matter of life or death."

"Looks like you weren't far off," I said. "Even so, don't call me at eight in the morning the next time." I hung up.

There was too much to think about for me to go back to sleep. I climbed wearily out of bed and made my way to the bathroom. A shower made me feel a little better, but not much. I forged through Jed's liquor stock and finally decided on some V.O. on the rocks. I carried it into the living room and started sipping at it.

I certainly didn't feel like working, but I was already stuck with the job. On the other hand, one percent of two and a half million dollars could finance a hell of a vacation. And the next time, I wouldn't leave a phone number. I finished the drink and made another one. By that time I was getting hungry. I looked in the refrigerator. There were eggs and ham and almost everything else you could think of. A fine friend, Jed. I put two slices of ham in a frying pan and went back to my second drink.

I was into my third, and starving, when the ham was ready. I added two eggs to the pan and put up some coffee. With two slices of bread in the toaster, the eggs once over lightly, breakfast was ready. I finished my drink, poured the coffee, and enjoyed my meal.

Fate could not harm me; I had dined that morning. I poured a second cup of coffee, added some brandy, and retired to the living room.

I had just finished when the doorbell rang. It was a Western Union messenger with a beautiful check for $2,000. I was so overcome that I gave him a five-dollar bill. Then I went back to the couch and gazed lovingly at the check. It inspired me to have another drink.

Maybe, I was thinking, I could have part work and part vacation, all on the expense account. Intercontinental couldn't expect me to work day and night, especially when there were so many uncalled phone numbers in Jed's black book.

Finally I went into the bathroom and shaved. Then I got dressed. As I came back into the living room, the phone rang. I picked it up and said hello.

"You March?" a man's voice asked.

I admitted I was.

"You're mixed up with a broad named Lita Harper," he said.

"Hardly. I barely know her. What about it?"

"You were with her last night. You had dinner with her and went around to the bars. Then she came back there and stayed with you until she went upstairs to knock off Johnny Renaldi."

"I had dinner and some drinks with her. I don't know what she did after she left me."

"You know," he said, "you're some kind of private dick, ain't you?"

"I've been called that. Who are you?"

"Never mind. I just want to tell you, if you have ideas, just forget them."

"Meaning what?"

"Don't try to pull any tricks to get the broad off. She's going to that gas chamber and I'm going to laugh while she's sitting in the chair."

"Why?"

"Johnny Renaldi was my friend. If the state don't take care of her, I will. And I don't want any smart guy from New York trying to louse things up."

"You sound like an outstanding citizen," I said. "Give me your name and I'll recommend that Chief Anderson* award you a medal."

"Keep your nose clean or you'll find out who I am," he said. There was a click as he hung up.

---

* Clinton H. Anderson was Beverly Hills Police Chief from 1942 to 1969. He had an exemplary career and investigated several famous cases, including the murder of mobster Bugsy Siegel. (All footnotes were added by the editor.)

THREE

This was an interesting situation. Lita Harper had practically been caught red-handed in the Renaldi murder. I had been what might be called a witness after the fact. That had been my only capacity until about three hours before this phone call. And now somebody was worried that I might do something to clear Lita. It brought up all sorts of possibilities.

I went out and drove to a Western Union office and cashed my Intercontinental check. The money produced a comfortable feeling in my pocket. It was still too early to go to the Beverly Hills police, so I drove slowly back up Sunset and went to the Scandia. I had a couple of martinis at the bar, enjoying them even more because Intercontinental was paying for them, then went into the dining room and had a leisurely and delicious lunch.

Finally I left the restaurant and drove to the Beverly Hills police department. I went in and asked for Lieutenant O'Brien. I was directed to an office. The Lieutenant was there, his desk piled high with papers. He looked tired but managed a smile as he looked up at me. "Hello, March," he said. "Sit down."

I took the chair next to his desk and lit a cigarette. "How are you, Lieutenant?"

"How do I look?" he asked sourly. "Are you ready to make a statement?"

"Yes."

"Good. The stenographer is on his way."

He had barely finished the sentence when there was a knock on the door and a young man came in carrying a stenographic shorthand machine. He sat down, a bored look on his face.

"Go ahead," the Lieutenant said.

I dictated my statement, sticking to what I knew and what I had seen. It didn't take too long. The young man got up and left, still looking bored.

"It'll be typed up in a few minutes and you can sign it and go," the Lieutenant said. "We'll expect you to be available for the trial."

"Sure," I said. "What about my gun?"

"It's clean." He opened a desk drawer and removed the gun. He handed it over to me. "Just don't go shooting anyone in Beverly Hills."

"Hollywood is all right?" I asked with a smile. I put the gun in my pocket. "What's the story so far?"

He gave me a sharp glance. "You're a witness for the prosecution. That doesn't entitle you to special information. In fact, it might influence your testimony."

"I'm more than a witness."

"What does that mean?"

"Since eight o'clock this morning, it's also my case. Lita Harper is insured by Intercontinental Insurance. At eight o'clock this morning I had a call from New York telling me to work on the case, since there is a time clause in connection with any cancellation."

"How much insurance?"

"Five hundred thousand dollars."

He whistled. "Well, that puts you on the other side of the fence and makes you a pretty poor witness."

"Not necessarily. I've already given you a statement, and that isn't changed even if she's innocent. I won't welch on the statement. But in the meantime, I have to work on the case. We can work at cross-purposes or we can cooperate. It's up to you."

"What do you mean by cooperate?"

"Just what I say. We exchange information."

"What's to exchange? We have a pretty clear case."

"Maybe," I said. "It may check out to be a true case. Then again, it may not. In that event, there can be a lot of exchange."

He smiled at me. "I sent through a request for information about you last night. I received an answer from the New York City police about an hour ago. Maybe you'd like to see it." He tossed a telegram across to me. I looked at it.

MILO MARCH WILL PICK YOUR BRAINS, STEAL YOUR IDEAS, THEN GO OUT AND SOLVE YOUR CASE, BUT HE WILL GIVE YOU THE CREDIT. HE'LL USE HIS OWN METHODS AND MIGHT EVEN BEND THE LAW, BUT OTHERWISE HE'S A RESPONSIBLE CITIZEN.

JOHN ROCKLAND (LT.)

I pushed the telegram back. "That sounds like Johnny. It just shows that it's a mistake to be friendly with a cop."

O'Brien laughed. "All right, I'll take a chance. The gun that Lita Harper was holding was the one that killed Johnny Renaldi. He was shot twice. One bullet went through his lungs and the other through his heart. The only clear prints on the gun were those of Lita Harper. The gun belonged to Renaldi. We have evidence that she had been seeing him pretty regularly for the past six months and often spent the night in his apartment. They also had a lot of quarrels, some in public and some in the apartment. The latter were overheard by neighbors. He had beaten her up a couple of times. Once she called us, but then dropped the charges."

"What's her story?" I asked gently.

"She says she didn't kill him. She claims that she was in the apartment with him when someone knocked on the door. He told her to get out of sight, and she went into the bedroom. A few minutes later, according to her, she heard two shots, and when she ran out he was on the floor, dead, and there was no one else in the room. She says that the gun was on the floor beside him and she picked it up without thinking—but they all say that. We finally got a statement out of her this morning. We couldn't get her to talk last night."

"May I see her?"

"Not now," he said, shaking his head. "Only her lawyer can see her at present. There will be a preliminary hearing immediately. Then she will be sent to the new county jail for women in Los Angeles* to wait for her trial. You'll be able to visit her there."

"All right," I said pleasantly. "You know, Lieutenant, I'm involved with more than just Lita Harper."

"What does that mean?"

---

* This new jail must be the Sybil Brand Institute in L.A. County. It opened in 1963 and closed in 1997.

"I understand that Johnny Renaldi was your prize suspect in another case. It must have been quite a blow when he was careless enough to get himself killed."

"Where did you hear that?"

"From New York. Intercontinental was carrying the insurance on a lot of that jewelry. Two million dollars' worth. They said that they understood from the Beverly Hills police that the only possible suspect they had was Johnny Renaldi. With him gone, they've decided to assign me to that case, too."

"The jewel robberies are not in my department. I'll work closely with Lieutenant Cooper because we believe that there may be some connection between the two cases, but your offer of cooperation in that case will have to be taken up with Lieutenant Cooper."

"I expected it to be another department. Is Lieutenant Cooper also in this building?"

"Yes. Lieutenant Fred Cooper. His office is two doors down the hall."

"Thank you, Lieutenant."

He looked at me and smiled. "I'll call and warn him you're coming." He picked up his phone and dialed three numbers. "Fred," he said, "Nathan. I have a private detective in my office. He's from New York, but he also has a California license. It seems he is interested in one of my cases and in one of yours. His name is Milo March and he says he's eager to cooperate with us. He wants to see you." He listened for a minute. "Frankly, I suspect he's part con man and part tough guy, but for a private detective he gets a good rating from the

New York police. … All right, Fred." He hung up and swung back to face me. "He'll see you for a few minutes."

"Thank you, Lieutenant," I said, standing up.

"One more thing, March. Are you going to continue living in that apartment?"

"That's the general idea. If my friend returns before I'm ready to go back to New York, I'll let you know where I'm moving."

"You do that. I want to be sure you're on tap. And if you learn anything, I expect you to come in here with it."

"Naturally," I said gravely. I went out and walked down to the second door, where I knocked, and a muffled voice told me to come in. I opened the door and stepped inside.

He was older than O'Brien, a big, rumpled man with gray hair. A half-smoked cigar was jammed in one corner of his mouth.

"Lieutenant Cooper?" I asked.

He nodded. "You're this Milo March?" he countered.

"I'm this Milo March."

"Sit down."

I took the chair next to his desk, glanced at his cigar, then took out a cigarette and lit it. I leaned back and waited for him to make the next move.

"So you're a private dick," he said finally.

"That's what it says on my license."

"I don't like private dicks," he said. "I don't like any kind of amateur cops."

That's fine," I said evenly. "But I think we ought to get a couple of things straight. Just because I don't wear a badge and don't have my feet in the public trough doesn't mean that I'm an amateur. I've been in this business a long time, with a little extra sharpening from the OSS and the CIA. I know my business and I've probably solved more cases than you have, but I don't throw my weight around about it. You don't have to flash a badge to be a professional."

"Are you through, lad?" he asked.

"I'm through about that."

He smiled around the cigar. "No offense, lad. I was just trying your mettle. Most of the private detectives we run into act as if they'd just crawled out of the woodwork. So you're going to solve a couple of our cases?"

"I didn't say that, Lieutenant. My company is interested in the solution of both cases, and if I can help in any way, I will do so. That is why I suggested cooperation."

He leaned back and chuckled. "Nathan says that the New York police think you're okay. I guess Nathan does too or he wouldn't have described you the way he did. So what's this cooperation you're asking for?"

"Just what it says. You have to work on the jewel case and so do I. It makes more sense if we trade information."

"Maybe. Who'd you say you worked for?"

"Intercontinental Insurance."

He nodded. "And what are you offering to trade?"

I smiled. "At the moment, nothing. I just got the assignment."

"Sounds like a one-sided trade."

"Not exactly. To start with, I think my company is entitled to a certain amount of information. I'm offering to keep in touch with you to exchange the results of future investigations."

"Well, it might be worth trying," he said, "but I'll have to be the judge of how much information we can give you."

"Naturally." I didn't bother to add that I expected to take the same attitude about information I gathered.

"And we will expect full cooperation from you."

"Of course," I said. "I might add, Lieutenant, that if I should contribute anything that will help solve the case, I will not expect any credit."

The cigar moved with his smile. "Wasn't expecting to give you any. What do you want to know, March?"

"Anything you feel you can tell me about the jewel robberies. I came out here yesterday on my vacation. This morning I received a phone call from the company putting me to work."

"Just starting your vacation, eh? Now, why would they do a thing like that?"

"Partly because I was on the scene, I imagine."

"Still, the jewelry robberies started a couple of months ago. I don't suppose that it had anything to do with the murder last night?"

"Partly that, too," I admitted. "We carry a fairly large policy on the woman who was arrested."

"Thought it was something like that. Maybe the victim was part of the reason, too?"

"Yes. The office mentioned that Renaldi was your only suspect."

"Well, I wouldn't go that far," he said. "We got a few other ideas. Your company carry all the insurance on the jewelry?"

"No, but they do stand to lose about two million. I haven't been to the local office yet, but I'll get a list of the robberies that involve us. I gather that you think all the jobs were pulled by the same people."

"I'm certain of it. The M.O. was exactly the same in every case. While we didn't have enough evidence to arrest him yet, we were positive that Johnny Renaldi was the leader. There had to be at least three or four people working with him, possibly more."

"Mind telling me about your other suspects?"

"I'm not ready to name anyone yet—except one." He gave me that crooked smile again. "How much insurance is your company carrying on the Harper woman?"

"Half a million."

"Well, I got an idea that she was part of the ring and that maybe was the motive for the murder."

"Lita Harper?" I said in real surprise. "I thought she was a very successful interior decorator."

"She is. I didn't mean that she did it for money."

"Then why? For kicks?"

"You don't know anything about the case, do you?" he asked.

"I told you I didn't."

"Or about Johnny Renaldi?"

"Only that he had a record."

"That he did," Lieutenant Cooper said grimly. "For almost anything you want to name. And he beat most of the raps. We are fortunate out here in that we haven't had as much of the Syndicate as some other parts of the country, but Johnny

Renaldi was part of what we do have. He was a handsome devil; that much I'll have to give him. He had a lot of success with the girls. One of them was Lita Harper."

"I had a hint of that."

"They were, as you might say," he continued, "shacked up for the past three months or so, although she was more careful than the others. She was seldom seen with him in public."

"What does shacking up have to do with the robbery?"

"Whoever pulled the jobs had to have sources of information. One thing needed was somebody who had access to big homes and could learn who had expensive jewelry and where they kept it. Who would be better for such a job than a woman who had decorated many of the most expensive homes in Beverly Hills?"

"How many interior decorators are there in Beverly Hills?" I asked gently.

"Too many," he said, "but how many of them were shacked up with Johnny Renaldi? Lita Harper. No one else."

"It's a good argument," I admitted. "But it won't stand by itself. You'd have to check out all the other interior decorators, as well as other people having access to those homes for any connection they may have had with Renaldi."

"We have," he said gently. "Renaldi had no similar connections. It is true that he had access to certain homes because of other women he has seen, but none of those homes were among those robbed."

"All right," I said. "Go ahead."

"He also needed more than access. First, he had to find out who had jewels worth going after. That involved someone like Lita Harper. I think she was the one, but I can't prove it. It could have been someone else. Secondly, he had to have someone who knew when the jewels would be at home and not in the vault. Most people keep their valuable jewelry in a bank vault, except when they want to wear them—and overnight or over the weekend after they have worn them."

"Someone in the bank?" I suggested.

"It would seem to be the obvious. Even more so since everyone who was robbed used the same bank. But everyone in that bank has been checked from the time they were born, and we have not uncovered a single lead. It must be there, but we haven't found it. We're still looking."

"What bank?"

"The Palm National Bank on Sunset. Your company could give you the name just as well. I'm sure that it's part of the policy."

"I imagine so," I said. "What else?"

"Thirdly, he had to have means of knowing that a specific family was out of the house on a night when the jewelry was in the home."

I nodded. "Any leads on that score?"

"Leads, yes. But I am not prepared to name them."

"There has to be a fourth element," I said. "Or was Renaldi an expert at breaking in and opening wall safes?"

He removed the cigar from his mouth, looked at it, and then dropped it into the ashtray. He took another cigar from his pocket and lit it. "Johnny Renaldi was guilty of a lot of crimes, but I doubt if he could even open a cigar box. So he must have had someone who could."

"Leads?"

"Not a one. We have files on Renaldi's association with killers, pimps, bookies, blackmailers, and narcotics pushers, but no one fits the safebreaker description. There is no doubt, however, that he had the connections to get such a man. We'll find him."

"That means four persons in addition to Renaldi?"

"Yes. And possibly a fifth. He may have already lined up a fence to handle the sale of the jewelry. That could be someone here or in Chicago or in New York—or any one of a dozen other cities. And you can be sure that there are others."

"Such as?"

"Johnny Renaldi was a part of the Syndicate, or the Mafia, if you prefer that name. He worked for them and was permitted certain personal rackets, such as this one. But if he was in trouble, he could get help—or if he did something wrong, he could be in trouble. Do you know anything about the Syndicate?"

"I've brushed up against them once or twice," I said mildly.

"Is that all?"

"All I can tell you now."

"I can add one thing," I said slowly, "although it doesn't lead anywhere yet. Not long after I got the assignment this morning, I received a phone call from a man who didn't name himself. He suggested that I forget any interest in Lita Harper if I wanted to stay alive."

"I gather that you think it has some meaning."

"Don't you?"

"Yes," he said slowly, "but I'd rather hear your opinion first."

"I think it's obvious. Despite all the evidence against Lita Harper, I believe it throws some doubt on her guilt. Somebody wants her to go to the gas chamber for the killing. Now, who could that be?"

He nodded. "There is an obvious answer, but there could be others. There is, however, another conclusion."

"I know. It had to be someone involved. If he isn't the murderer, he is at least part of the jewel gang."

"Any idea who he is?"

"No. But he'll call me again. I'll see to that. It's the one way I can function better than the police."

"What do you mean?"

"I can keep pushing until someone makes a mistake. You can push, too, but not in the same way."

"Okay," he said, "you push your way and we'll push in ours. If you pick up anything, be sure to come in."

"I'll be dropping around," I told him with a smile. I snubbed out my cigarette and left.

I drove over to the Intercontinental office on Wilshire and introduced myself. I was shown into the office of a bright young man who had obviously received instructions about me. He wasted no time handing me the files on the cases with which we were involved. He invited me to use his office and disappeared. I couldn't tell whether he was merely glad to get rid of the cases or was anxious for a coffee break. I didn't worry about it.

I started going through the files. Intercontinental had insured the jewelry in six cases. There was a Mr. and Mrs. William Grant insured for $500,000; a Mr. and Mrs. Herman

Baines insured for $350,000; a Miss Kitty Mills insured for $300,000; Mr. and Mrs. Carl Carleton insured for $400,000; Mr. and Mrs. Thomas Ray insured for $250,000; and Miss Pamela Perry insured for $200,000. All of them lived in Beverly Hills.

Grant was a stockbroker. Baines was an attorney. So was Carleton. Ray was a realtor. Kitty Mills was an actress, and Pamela Perry was an agent. Obviously, all of them were successful.

There were other interesting similarities. All of them were insured with us. All of them usually kept their jewelry in the vaults of the Palm National Bank. They had been robbed on different nights, but in the case of each robbery, the individuals had been having dinner at the same restaurant: the Suckling Pig on the Sunset Strip. All of them had servants, but they had been off on the night of the robberies.

All of them were regular customers at the Suckling Pig. Emile Thoret was the headwaiter there, and was well known by all of them. It sounded like dozens of other restaurants and customers.

That was about the end of the similarities. Baines and Carleton knew each other casually, but that was all. There was apparently no other connection between any of them.

According to the files, there was no evidence that any of them had ever had any contact with Johnny Renaldi. Lita Harper was not mentioned. I made notes from the files and left. I found the bright young man having an intimate conversation with the receptionist. I took a second look at her and decided that he wasn't as stupid as he looked.

"Thank you," I told him. "I return your office to you just as it was, except for a small amount of cigarette smoke." I looked at the girl. "I must have been upset when I came in. I didn't realize that Intercontinental kept all of its assets in the reception room."

"Thank you," she said.

"Don't thank me, honey," I said, "I didn't have anything to do with it—yet." I winked at her and left.

I checked the time and decided it was too late to visit the clients. So I drove downtown, switching over to Hollywood Boulevard as soon as I got below Highland. When I reached Western Avenue, I drove into a parking lot and went into a bar on the corner. It was two years since I'd been there, but I was sure I would find the man I was looking for.

I didn't see him when I entered, but then I couldn't see anything. It was too dark in the place. Finally I made out the owner behind the bar.

"Hi, boss," I said. "Why don't you pay the light bill so we can see who's here?"

He recognized me. "Hi, partner," he said. "Where have you been?"

"On vacation," I said. It was my own private joke. "Bourbon and water backed."

He poured the drink and put a glass of water in front of me. "It must be a year or more," he said.

"Yeah," I said. "Is Big Joe still around?"

"Sure. He's in and out. Should be back in a minute." He pushed my money toward me. "Welcome back."

"Thanks, Mike," I said.

I lifted my glass to him and drank. I ordered another one for myself and one for him, then sipped the second drink and waited. It was another five minutes before Big Joe came in.

He was Joe Larson, and he was big, four or five inches over six feet, and heavy. He was in his sixties and had been around since the rackets in Chicago during Prohibition. You might say he was retired now, but he knew pretty much what was going on. He came into the bar looking as if he were trying to catch a train, and went by without even seeing me.

"Been to the track, Joe?" someone asked.

"Yeah," he grunted.

"How did you do?"

"Down the drain. I couldn't even pick my own father out of a lineup."

Everyone laughed and Joe went over to sit at the piano bar on the other side of the room. I ordered another drink for myself and one for him and carried them both over to where he sat.

"Hello, Joe," I said, putting the drinks down.

He peered at me, then his face lit up. "Hi, buddy," he said. "Haven't seen you in a year or so. When did you get in town?"

"Yesterday. It was supposed to be a vacation."

"Looking for a girl? Stay away from most of them around here. There are a couple who are dandies, but most of them have been jumped so often they're canvasbacks. But let's see …"

"I said it was supposed to have been a vacation," I interrupted. "It changed this morning. I'm working again. And I'm looking for some information."

"What kind?"

"Know a hood named Johnny Renaldi?"

"Yeah. A punk. Somebody killed him last night."

"I know. That's why my vacation is over. What do you know about him?"

"He's a no-good punk and a pimp."

"I need more than that, Joe," I said gently. "Who were his friends?"

"More punks. The mob."

"Who?"

"He always hung around Mickey Bronson's gang."

"Where?"

"They usually are at the Pink Whistle on Sunset."

"Who was Renaldi close to?"

"Danny Polerri and Little Benjy Macklin."

"What do they do?"

"They're hoods."

"No," I said, "I mean do they have specialties?"

"Little Benjy is a muscleman, and Danny is a gun and a heist artist."

"Can either one of them open a safe?"

He thought for a minute. "No, but there is a guy in the gang who can. Mack Larry."

"Okay. Thanks, Joe."

"Are you going to the Pink Whistle?"

"I might drop in."

"Want me to go along and cover your back?"

"I don't think it's necessary now," I said. "Thanks for the offer."

"Anytime," he said. "Are you looking for the guy who dusted Renaldi?"

"Maybe. I'm not sure yet. I'll look around first."

He nodded. "There's a broad at the Pink Whistle. She's one of the strippers. Peaches Pratt. She was part of Renaldi's stable for a while. She's been passed around so much she has dribble marks on her bottom, but remember that she's a smart broad."

"I'll try," I told him.

I finished my drink, said I'd see him, and left. I got in the Cadillac and drove west until I saw a restaurant that looked good. I went in, had a couple of martinis, and then a good dinner. It was still too early when I finished, so I drove to Sunset Boulevard and stopped in another bar for a couple of slow drinks.

Finally, I got back into the car and drove up Sunset until I came to the Pink Whistle. I turned the car over to the parking attendant and went inside. I had nothing in mind, particularly, but it wouldn't hurt to take a look at the place.

By parting with some of Intercontinental's money, I got a table near the stage and ordered a drink. I was already on the second drink when the floor show finally started. There were the usual dreary number of strippers who went through mechanical contortions with fixed expressions on their faces. After three or four of these there was a change in the music, and I opened my eyes again. Peaches Pratt came on the stage.

She wasn't much better as a performer, but her face was alive and she possessed a sensuality that was electrifying. I joined in the applause as she left the stage. The lights came on.

I ordered another drink and looked around. The place was packed, but my attention soon centered on a table near me. There were three men seated at it, looking as if they owned the club. Two of them were small, dapper men and the third was a huge man who was bulging out of his suit at every possible point.

I attracted the attention of my waiter. "I wonder," I said mildly, "if you could tell me who the three gentlemen are at the second table behind you?"

"That," he said, without looking around, "is Mr. Polerri and his party."

"Oh," I said, "I thought one of them was a movie star. Thank you." He moved away, but a little later I noticed he stopped by that table and said something. They all laughed, but then they began to show some interest in me.

I had a couple more drinks and then called for the check, gave the waiter some money, and left. "Would you get my car?" I asked the attendant. "It's a white Cadillac."

He didn't look at me. "I'm waiting for an important guest," he muttered. "Would you mind getting it for yourself? It's in the back of the lot. The keys are in it."

"Thanks," I said dryly.

I walked back through the cars until I spotted mine. I had almost reached it when three men stepped out from behind another car. They were the men who had been sitting at the second table. One of them held a gun. It was pointed at me.

FOUR

We stood looking at each other for at least a minute. I was cursing under my breath. My gun was in the car instead of being strapped on my left side as it should have been. And I had made a mistake in not getting suspicious when the attendant refused to get my car. I don't make mistakes very often. It's not a good idea in my business.

"What is this?" I asked. "A stick-up?"

"A funny guy," one of them said. "I told you March would make some kind of crack when we stopped him."

"You know me?" I asked in pretended surprise.

"We know you, March. What were you doing in the Pink Whistle?"

"Is that all?" I asked. I recognized his voice. He was the man who had phoned me that morning. "I was driving up Sunset looking for a place to have a few drinks and see a show. The name of the place interested me and I stopped. That's all. Did I stumble into a private club?"

"Yeah, you might say that. Little Benjy, show him he ain't supposed to stick his nose into things that ain't none of his business."

The big man lumbered toward me, his hands swinging like two clubs. While I didn't look forward to tangling with him, I was relieved. The plan was apparently to beat me up and not to shoot me. Watching Benjy closely, I began to back up toward my car. He just kept coming at the same pace with no change in his expression.

"What's wrong, March?" one of the other men said. "I thought you were a tough guy. Little Benjy won't hurt you—much." He laughed as though he thought he'd just said something witty. Maybe he had.

I decided to try Little Benjy once for size. I stopped and waited. When he was near enough, he swung one of those fists. I stepped inside of it and swung as hard as I could—hoping that he had a glass jaw. He didn't. I could feel the blow all the way to my shoulder, but he just grunted and reached for me with his left hand. I backed quickly out of the way.

This time I didn't stop until I reached a spot next to the door of my car. If there was any final play to be made, this was the spot. I guessed that the parking attendant had been paid to make sure there were no interruptions. It was strictly up to me.

I didn't wait for him to swing. I stepped forward and hit him just below the ribs. It was like shoving my fist into a concrete wall. Then it was his turn. Before I could get out of the way, he caught me high on the cheek. It felt like I'd been hit by a two-by-four. Part of my face went numb, and there was a warm trickle down my cheek as I fell backward to the ground. *You'd better think of something fast, Milo,* I told myself.

I looked up from the ground and saw his foot swinging at me. I rolled to one side, grabbed his foot, and heaved as hard as I could. For a brief moment he towered above me, tottering on his feet; then he went down like an axed tree. He hit almost as hard as one. His breath whistled as it was forced from his lungs. I didn't waste any time looking at him. I jerked open the car door and threw myself inside.

"Hold it, March," the man with the gun called.

Out of the corners of my eyes I saw Little Benjy getting to his feet as I twisted the ignition key. The motor roared into life. I threw it into gear and stepped on the accelerator. The tires screamed as the car jumped forward. The door swung shut, hitting Little Benjy and knocking him down again. I kept pushing on the gas as I threaded my way through the parked cars.

There was the sound of a gunshot behind me, but nothing happened, so I kept on going. I was doing about fifty by the time I reached the street entrance to the restaurant. I got some small pleasure from the fact that the attendant had to leap out of the way. I braked fast just before hitting the street, swerved into the main stream of traffic, and was cursed for it. I watched the rearview mirror but didn't see another car leaving the restaurant, so I concentrated on getting home.

It was only a few minutes before I reached the apartment building. I parked the car, got my gun from the glove compartment, and waited. No one followed me into the street. Finally I climbed out and went into the building. I tossed the gun on the couch and went into the bathroom.

My cheek was cut and the side of my face was covered with drying blood. I turned on the cold water and carefully washed off the blood. The cut wasn't bad, not much more than an inch long. I washed it with soap and water, scrubbing until the blood started seeping from it again. I dug through the medicine cabinet until I found something to put on it, then covered it with a bandage. I took another look at my face. A good-sized bruise was already puffing it up.

I stopped in the kitchen and made myself a stiff drink and carried it into the other room. Tossing my jacket on a chair, I sat down to nurse the drink and my aching cheek.

There seemed to be only one conclusion I could reach about what had just happened. Somebody wanted Lita Harper to be convicted for the murder of Johnny Renaldi, and the same somebody was afraid I might have a different idea. He might or might not know that I was also involved in trying to recover the missing jewelry. Whatever he thought, it was clear that he wanted to discourage my activities.

Something else occurred to me. O'Brien had said that Renaldi was part of the Syndicate. I had tangled with them a few times, so even though I had never seen the three men before, they might already know a few things about me.

Finally, I decided there was nothing more I could do at the moment. I turned on the television set, made myself another drink, and leaned back to relax. Several drinks later I muttered good night to Mr. Carson and went to bed.

I was up early the next morning. My cheek was an interesting array of colors. It hurt some when I shaved, but felt better after my shower. I made some ham and eggs and had a good breakfast. Then I got dressed, remembering to strap on my shoulder holster and slip the gun into it. I wasn't going to be taken by surprise again. I went out and drove to the police station. I was sent right back to O'Brien's office. He looked up as I entered.

"Run into something?" he asked.

"Yeah," I said. I sat in the chair next to his desk. "Something called Little Benjy—although where the hell they got the 'Little' from I'll never know."

"Benjy Macklin," he said. He smiled. "And that's all you got out of it? You were lucky."

"Thanks. I knew I was something, but I hadn't actually thought of it in those terms."

"I see you're a little more fully dressed today. Expecting a return encounter?"

"Maybe. I left rather hurriedly last night, and they may feel that their business with me wasn't finished."

He leaned back in his chair. "Care to tell me about it? Listening to the problems of our citizens is part of my job."

"You're all heart, Lieutenant," I told him. "It's really very simple. I asked some questions about Renaldi and was told that his friends often hang out in a nightclub on Sunset."

"The Pink Whistle," he said, nodding. "I could've told you that. You should've asked."

"I was always told not to be too forward with strange men," I said primly. "So you know Little Benjy?"

"I know him."

"How about his friends?"

"Which ones?"

"Well, I heard about a Danny Polerri. Then maybe a Mickey Bronson or a Mack Larry."

"Were they there last night?"

"I'm not sure about one of them. There were three men at a table near mine. One of them was Little Benjy and one was Polerri. I don't know who the other one was."

"Did he look like a slightly fat bulldog?"

"No. He was about the same size as Polerri."

"Then it wasn't Mickey. Maybe it was Larry, although he doesn't usually go in for rough stuff."

"He didn't last night either. Polerri held a gun on me, and both of them were going to watch Little Benjy give me my lumps. Incidentally, you might be interested in knowing that I recognized Polerri's voice. He was the man who called me yesterday morning."

"Tell me what happened."

"I've already told you most of it. They were sitting a couple of tables away from me. I thought that they looked like hoods, and I asked the waiter who they were. He said Mr. Polerri and his party. I said something about thinking one of them was a movie star and let it go at that."

"Then the waiter tipped them off?"

"Probably. He stopped at their table after a time. It wasn't much later when I decided to leave. When I got outside, the parking attendant said he couldn't get my car just then, but I could go back and get it myself."

"The waiter probably gave him his orders."

"I could figure that out for myself," I said sourly. "Just as I can figure out that the three of them went through the kitchen and out the back way while I was talking to the attendant. Anyway, they were there waiting for me when I got near my car. Polerri with the gun called me by name and said that Little Benjy was going to teach me not to stick my nose in things that weren't my business."

"He called you by name? How'd he know who you were?"

"I don't know. But he knew where I was staying, and he might have followed me sometime yesterday. I wasn't checking to see if I had a tail."

"Trusting of you," he said with a smile. "Go ahead."

"Well, the trained ape started for me and I began to back off toward my car. By this time I had figured out that Polerri probably wouldn't shoot, so my chief worry was Little Benjy. He was enough. I stopped once to see if he had a glass jaw and damn near broke my hand. But finally I upset him. While he was down, I scrambled into the car and got out of there as fast as the car could make it. Polerri snapped one shot after me, but that was all."

"Where was your gun?"

"In the glove compartment, where I'd put it after picking it up from you."

"Want to make charges against them?" he asked.

I shook my head. "No. I'll be ready for them if they try again."

"I wouldn't say that they are among our most valuable citizens, but we still take a dim view of dead bodies scattered around the city. Our citizens think it's untidy."

"I'll remember that," I said gravely. "If anyone tries to shoot me in Beverly Hills, I'll carefully lead the killer into Los Angeles and then defend myself."

He laughed. "Thanks for telling me about it, March. What do you make of it?"

"I told you yesterday. Somebody is anxious to make sure that Lita Harper goes up for the murder of Renaldi. Who seems to be the most anxious? And who would have the most reason to be anxious? Obviously, someone who did have something to do with the murder."

"Maybe," he said. "On the other hand, it might just be someone who is interested in the stolen jewelry and sees this merely as a convenient way not to have to hand out two shares of the loot."

"I don't believe it," I said. "You have anything new, Lieutenant?"

"No, but we're working on it."

"Sure, but don't forget that 'cooperation' is the keyword. Will I be permitted to see Miss Harper today?"

"I imagine so, but you'd better check with her lawyer. He says he doesn't want anyone seeing her except in his presence."

"Who is he?"

"Mortimer Harrison. He has offices here in Beverly Hills."

"Okay. Thanks, Lieutenant. I'll drop in on you again."

"I'm sure you will." He smiled at me. "Thanks for coming in, March. As soon as we have more information, I'll fill you in on anything that seems pertinent to your case."

"And I'll do the same," I muttered as I left.

I found the nearest place to make a phone call and looked up Mortimer Harrison. I dialed his number, and a secretary finally put me through to him.

"This is Milo March," I repeated, in case he hadn't heard my name correctly.

"Oh, yes, Mr. March," he said. "Lieutenant O'Brien did mention that you might phone me. What can I do for you?"

"I want to see Miss Harper."

"Well, I'm not so sure about that, Mr. March. I understand that you are a witness for the prosecution."

I took a deep breath. "Mr. Harrison, when this case eventually comes to trial, I imagine I will be a witness for the prosecution, but I do not believe that Miss Harper will be there."

"Eh? What do you mean?"

"I do not believe that Miss Harper killed Johnny Renaldi. It will be one of my jobs to find out who did. I will need all the help I can get."

"What do you mean it's one of your jobs?"

"I guess the Lieutenant didn't tell you everything about me. I'm an investigator for Intercontinental Insurance. They carry a policy on Miss Harper for half a million dollars. They take a dim view of paying out that sort of money unless they can't avoid it. So if someone else killed Renaldi, they very much want me to find him."

"I see. You say that is part of your job. What is the rest of it?"

"There is a large amount of jewelry missing. It was also insured by my company. There is some belief that Johnny Renaldi was involved in the theft of the jewelry. It would seem that one of his partners might have been interested in removing him from among the living. Now may I see Miss Harper?"

"Your story does change the picture somewhat," he said slowly. There was a pause. "Do you know where the county jail for women is located?"

"I can find it."

"Very well. I will meet you there in two hours." He hung up before I could say anything more.

I drove back into Hollywood and stopped at the bar on

the corner of Western Avenue. Big Joe was there in his usual place. I took a stool at the regular bar and ordered a drink. After it was served, Big Joe came over.

"Who hung one on you?" he asked.

"Fellow by the name of Little Benjy."

"I told you I should go with you," he said. "Did you shoot him?"

"No. My gun was in the glove compartment of my car."

"If you need any help, you'll let me know?"

"Sure. But I'm more prepared today."

"I noticed. Why weren't you carrying the piece yesterday?"

"I'd just picked it up from the cops and didn't have my holster with me, so I put it in the car. But I'll be ready for them if they want a return engagement."

"Okay, buddy." He slapped me on the back and left.

A little later I left and drove downtown. I put the car in a parking lot and went over to the jail. I found the place to check in for a visit.

A uniformed guard came up to me. "You want to see someone?" he asked.

"Yes," I said. "But I'm waiting for an attorney, Mortimer Harrison."

"Okay," he said. He looked at me sharply, then suddenly poked a finger at my left shoulder. At the same time I was aware that another man had moved up behind me.

"A present for a prisoner?" the first guard asked.

"Get a scriptwriter if you want to make jokes," I told him. "It's a gun. I intended to check it with you before going inside to see anyone."

"Sure, you did," he said. He reached inside my coat and pulled out the gun. "Well, isn't that a pretty one. I suppose you have the legal right to carry this around with you?"

"I do. Do you want me to show it to you or do you prefer to paw around for it yourself?"

He had my gun, so he felt brave. "Show me. Only don't make any fast moves."

"Who needs the exercise?" I asked.

I reached into my coat and produced my ID case. I flipped it open to the right card and held it out. The guard took it and looked at the picture. Finally, he returned it.

"You visiting a prisoner?"

"Yes. With her attorney when he arrives."

"Okay. We'll keep the gun until you leave."

"Fine," I said, "just give me a receipt for it. That will still give you plenty of time to check it out before I'm finished."

He didn't like that, but he turned the gun over to another guard and told him to give me a receipt for it. I waited patiently until I received it, then moved out of the way.

A few minutes later a tall, gray-haired man entered. He looked around and then came over to me, since I was the only civilian there.

"Mr. March?" he asked uncertainly.

"Yes."

"Mortimer Harrison," he announced. We shook hands briefly. "This is most unusual, but I am inclined to believe that you may be of some assistance to my client. I trust that I am not making a mistake."

"I told you my position. You could easily check on it."

"To tell you the truth," he said uneasily, "I did speak to your superiors at Intercontinental Insurance. They speak very highly of you. We'll see Miss Harper in just a minute."

He walked over to the desk and a moment later nodded to me.

A guard escorted us into a small room just inside the cell-block. He left us there. It was a bare room with three chairs and a battered desk.

A couple of minutes later the door opened and a police-woman escorted Lita Harper into the room, then left and closed the door. Lita looked at me and managed a wan smile.

"Hello, Milo," she said.

"Hello, Lita," I replied gravely. I moved over and held the chair behind the desk. "This is for you, honey. Cigarette?"

"Please," she said.

I handed her a cigarette and held a light for her. Then I went back to my chair. They were both looking at me. I lit a cigarette for myself.

"Mr. Harrison," I said, "I am going to make a request which I am sure will distress you. I would like to talk to Miss Harper alone."

His face turned pink and he cleared his throat. "It is a most unusual request, Mr. March," he said finally. "It is my duty to stay with my client when she is questioned by anyone."

"I know," I said. "I can assure you that I will do nothing improper. It is possible that I will bring up subjects which are not directly related to your case, but which it would be better if you didn't hear. Anything I say about Miss Harper can be related to you. Don't forget that my company stands to lose a lot of money if I don't help her."

"It's highly irregular," he said. He stopped and looked at her.

"Please, Mr. Harrison," she said. "I would like to talk to Milo. I promise that I won't do anything that will distress you."

"Very well," he said with dignity. He stood up. "I will leave you alone for a few minutes." He turned and left the room.

I looked at her. "Hi, honey."

She managed another smile. "Hi, Milo. I'm sorry about the date."

I shrugged. "It wasn't really a date. I invited you to dinner and we had a very good time. Where you went later was your business."

"Okay," she said. This time she managed a real smile. "You told me that you run errands for a vice-president. What's this errand?"

"I still run errands for a vice-president. I'm a special investigator for Intercontinental Insurance, and they carry a small policy on you, so you're innocent of the charge against you. But you were before I knew you were a case."

"Thanks, Milo," she said. She made a vague gesture with her hands. "What do you want me to say?"

"Nothing special. You and Johnny Renaldi were a thing, right?"

"We were a thing," she said. Her voice sounded dead. "I knew it was no good from the beginning and it was really over, but something made me try to end it neatly. Don't ask me why. I don't know. Call it pride if you like."

"I don't have to put a label on it," I said. "I don't need a history. Just tell me what happened."

"I've already told it twice and nobody believes me."

"I'll believe you, honey."

She took a deep breath. "Well, I went upstairs and knocked on Johnny's door when I left you. He was there and alone. He—he thought I was going to spend the night there, but I started telling him that I wasn't going to see him anymore. We were still talking about it when there was a knock on the door. Johnny told me to get into the bedroom and close the door and keep quiet. I did, and a moment later I could hear him talking to someone, but I couldn't hear what was being said."

"Man or woman?"

"A man."

"Did you recognize his voice?"

She shook her head. "I don't think I'd ever heard it before. But then I never saw any of the people Johnny knew."

"Did you know that he had a criminal record?"

"Yes. Johnny told me about it. He seemed to be proud of it. I guess that's when I should have run."

"Go on, Lita."

"When I found out I couldn't hear what they were saying, I went over and sat on the bed, wishing that I had let you take me straight home. Suddenly I heard Johnny shout something, but I couldn't understand what it was. Then there were two quick shots. They sounded as if they came from a cannon." Her breath caught in her throat and she paused for a second before going on. "The next sound I heard was a heavy thud. I—I guess it was Johnny falling to the floor. Then there was something that sounded like the door closing. After that I couldn't hear anything. I don't know how long it was before

I got up enough nerve to open the door. The first thing I saw was Johnny—lying on the floor."

I waited until she recovered from that memory. "Was he dead?"

"I think so. I could see the blood all over his shirt, and he wasn't moving. I know that I thought he was dead."

"What did you do?"

"I screamed. I remember that I thought my throat was going to tear. But I don't remember much after that."

"What about the gun?" I asked gently.

"It—it was on the floor beside Johnny. I think I remember picking it up, but I'm not certain. I'm sorry, Milo, but everything is like a fuzzy nightmare from the time I screamed."

"It's all right," I said. I gave her another cigarette and took one myself, then lit them both. "I want to ask you some other questions, Lita. I must tell you that they are the reason I asked to see you without your attorney being present. I should also tell you that I am certain he would advise you not to answer them. On the other hand, I need to know some other answers if I am going to help you."

"What kind of answers, Milo?" she asked. She sounded very young and frightened.

"The killing of Johnny Renaldi," I said carefully, "is not an isolated act. It is related to something else—in which I am also interested. I don't think the two cases can be separated. I need to know about both of them if I am going to be of help in both."

There was another long silence.

"What do you mean?" she asked finally.

"I think you know what I mean, Lita," I said. "The police know, although they may not have questioned you about the second case yet. There is no question in their minds—or mine—that the murder of Renaldi is connected with a series of jewel robberies in Beverly Hills. The police think—and again I agree with them—that you are somehow implicated in the jewel thefts. I would like you to tell me what you know about them. I think I can promise you it will help you."

She managed a smile. "Are you asking me to give you a confession?"

"In a way I suppose so. But let's look at it realistically. You are already charged with murder. I believe that you are not guilty of that charge. But there will be another charge, either made openly or introduced in evidence to support the first charge. I need to know as much as possible to help you. I might be able to dig it all up, but if you can supply any information fast it will help."

"Information that you can take to the police?"

"No. It is true that once you go to trial, I will have to tell what I know. But it's not as bad as that sounds. I'm sure you are not a murderer; I am not so sure that you aren't involved in the robberies. However, even there I can be of some assistance, so you might get off more easily."

She thought about it for a minute. "Well, I've trusted you this far. I might as well go all the way. I was involved in the jewel robberies, but I didn't mean to be and I didn't even know I was until it was too late."

"What happened?"

"It's an old story," she said bitterly. "I thought Johnny was the greatest thing I'd ever met, and I was sure that with a good woman he would straighten out. I was going to be that good woman. That was a gasser." She laughed, but it was more like a sob. "Anyway, Johnny used to ask me about my work. He always wanted to know about the houses I had decorated, including such things as where the wall safes were and what kind of jewelry the women had. I let myself believe that he was interested in what I did. It was only later, when I read about the robberies, that I realized there had to be some connection."

"What did you do then?"

"I asked Johnny about it and he just laughed at me. I kept on asking and he finally told me that it was true about the robberies and his questioning me, but that if I tried to do anything about it I would go to jail."

"A nice boy," I said. "Who else was in on it?"

"I don't know. Honest, Milo. Johnny admitted to me that he was part of the robbery gang, but he never told me who else was. And several times I knew that he couldn't have broken into the houses himself, because he was with me."

"You never saw any of his partners?"

"Not that I know of."

"He never said anything about them?"

"No." She frowned. "Well, he did say something once, but it didn't mean anything. One night, when I met him, he kept laughing all the time. When I asked him why, he said some-body was trying to be a wise guy and grab a job for himself, but that he was going to be in for a surprise. That was the night he was in such good humor that he promised me a trip around the world when this was all over."

"Did he say when?"

"I asked him. He laughed again and said that we'd take off on the day that the stars came down from the sky like rain. But that was all I could get out of him. He'd just laugh when I asked what he meant."

"It doesn't seem to help very much," I agreed. "Anything else?"

"No, Milo. He never really told me anything about what he did. He would make vague references to friends, but never by name, and he never let me meet any of them."

"Have the police questioned you about the jewel robberies?"

"No."

"They will. They already think you're implicated, and they'll be around to ask you about it sooner or later. Discuss it with your attorney, but if I were you, I'd tell them the truth—just the way you told it to me."

"All right, Milo."

"Okay, honey," I said. I smiled at her. "Keep your chin up. I'll see what I can do."

I went over and opened the door. The attorney was standing just outside.

"Sorry to take so long," I told him, "but she's all yours now."

"This is highly irregular," he said stiffly.

"I know, but so is being locked up." I slapped him on the shoulder and left him standing there.

A guard stepped forward to let me out. I stopped by the counter and presented my receipt. Another guard gave me my gun and had me sign for it.

"All clean?" I asked cheerfully.

"Yeah," he grunted. He sounded unhappy.

"Cheer up," I told him, "there'll be a hot one along sometime, and then you can sit around and tell your grandchildren about the day that Grandpa stopped a desperate criminal from breaking into the women's jail." I slipped the gun into my holster and left.

Downstairs I got the Cadillac out of the parking lot and headed west. I skipped the freeway, since I couldn't take it very far, and drove along Sunset, thinking about the case. I hadn't learned very much from Lita Harper, but I still didn't believe she had committed murder.

I hadn't been paying much attention to anything, and I was in Hollywood before I spotted it. Just to make sure, I switched over to Santa Monica Boulevard and drove until I came to a bar. I parked and went inside. I had a drink and got a package of cigarettes from the machine. Then I went out to my car and drove off.

A black Ford pulled away from the curb right behind me. It was the same one I now realized was following me before. The driver was the only person in it. I couldn't see what he looked like.

FIVE

One thing was reassuring. It seemed obvious that he wasn't trying to find a place to jump me right away. If he wanted to just trail around to see where I was going, that was all right for the time being. I settled back and paid more attention to driving.

My next stop was the building where Intercontinental had their offices. I noticed that my shadow parked not far behind me, but I didn't even glance at him as I entered the building.

I found a secretary in Intercontinental who agreed to run off a copy of the description of the jewels stolen from our clients with the names and addresses of the victims. She said it would take only a few minutes. I took advantage of the time to borrow the use of their direct-line telephone to call the New York office. Martin Raymond came on the phone at once.

"Milo, boy," he exclaimed, "how are things going?"

"The way things always go," I said. "I just came from talking to your half-million-dollar baby."

"You mean Miss Harper?"

"That was the general idea."

"How does it look?"

"I don't think she committed the murder. Now all I have to do is prove she didn't."

"Do you think you can, Milo?" he asked anxiously.

"I'd better—at the rates you're paying. If I do, it'll save you the half million on her policy, and it may give you the excuse to cancel the policy shortly thereafter."

"What do you mean?"

"Well, she was playing house with the guy who was killed. And I think that she was involved to some extent in the robberies."

"My God," he said. There was a pause. "Well, do your best, Milo."

"Don't I always?" I muttered. "How many robberies were there?"

"Haven't you seen the records there? Six of our policies are involved, totaling two million dollars."

"I don't mean that, Martin. Were only Intercontinental policies involved, or were other insurance companies hit?"

"Others were hit too. I don't know how many, but I understand Excelsior Mutual was clipped for more than we were."

"Has any of the jewelry shown up or any approach been made to any of the insurance companies?"

"Not so far as I know."

"Okay," I said. "If I run out of drinking money I'll let you know."

"I'm sure you will," he said sourly, and hung up.

I went out and collected the descriptions the girl had made for me. When I reached the lobby of the building, I looked out at the street. The black Ford was still parked behind my car and a man still sat behind the steering wheel. I walked down the street. When I reached my car, I tossed the envelope onto the seat and kept on walking. As I neared the Ford, I could see that the driver was Danny Polerri, the man who'd held a gun on me and told Little Benjy to beat me up. I looked around while I was still walking. There were no cops in sight.

As I drew even with the Ford, I took my gun from the holster. Then I suddenly turned to the car, ducked down, and put my head inside. The gun was pointed at his middle. He had already started to reach for the ignition key, but jerked his hand back at sight of the gun.

"Hello, Danny," I said.

"I don't know you," he said sullenly.

"Sure, you know me, Danny. You held a gun on me last night while Little Benjy was supposed to beat me to a pulp. Why are you following me?"

"I'm not following you. I'm just sitting here, waiting for a friend."

"Sure. Let your friend take a bus and you get out of here. Just start driving up the street and keep going. I don't like anyone looking over my shoulder, especially a crumb like you."

"You can't tell me what to do," he said. "You don't dare to try to shoot me in the middle of Beverly Hills like this."

"Sure, I do. I've already reported your one attempt. You're carrying a gun and you're a hood. All I have to do is swear that you tried to draw your gun and I shot in self-defense. You're not going to testify, so that will be the official record." I paused long enough to let that sink in. "But I won't shoot you unless you go for your gun. What I will do is drag you out of the car and pistol-whip you. Take your choice, Danny. Start moving or ..."

The unfinished sentence hung there for a moment, then he reached over and turned the ignition key. The motor roared to life.

"I'll get you for this, March," he said. "So help me, I will."

He threw the car into gear and swerved out from the curb, ignoring the traffic. There was a screech of brakes from an oncoming car, but he made it. I put my gun away and watched him as he went up the street. I waited until he had gone at least ten blocks without turning, then walked back to my car. I pulled out and turned right at the first intersection. I made several more turns just as a precaution. There was no one behind me, so I straightened out and headed for another part of Beverly Hills.

My first stop was at the address listed for Mr. and Mrs. Carl Carleton. Stolen jewelry, including rings, bracelets, necklaces, pins, and loose diamonds, insured for $400,000. Mr. Carleton was listed as an attorney.

It was a nice little shack, no more than twenty rooms and about five acres of ground, plus a swimming pool and tennis courts. I walked up to the front door and rang the bell. After a moment the door opened and a maid looked out.

"Good afternoon," I said. "I would like to see either Mrs. Carleton or Mr. Carleton, or both if that is possible."

She looked doubtful. "Whom shall I announce?"

"Mr. Milo March. Tell them I represent the Intercontinental Insurance Company."

"I do not think they wish to see insurance salesmen …"

"I do not think that I wish to sell them any insurance," I said gravely. "If there is any question, they already have insurance with my company, and they are expecting us to pay them on a policy. When they get the money depends on when they see me."

That shook her up. "Just a moment," she said, and left, closing the door in my face.

But she was back so soon that I was certain she hadn't had to look through all twenty rooms.

"This way, Mr. March," she said.

I followed her—which afforded me such a pleasant view I almost forgot why I was there. We ended up in something that appeared to be a library. A man and woman were there. They both looked as if they had a lot of money and had invested most of it in their stomachs.

"Mr. March," the maid said, and beat a hasty retreat.

"March," the man echoed in a voice that was slightly theatrical. He stood up and held out his hand. "I'm Carl Carleton. This is Mrs. Carleton."

"Mrs. Carleton," I murmured. Then I shook his hand. "I'm glad you're home, Mr. Carleton. I thought I ought to arrange to come at another time in order to be sure of catching you here. But I took a chance."

"Glad you did," he said. He was just a little too amiable, but that was the sort of miracle that $400,000 can create in people—even rich ones. "I just got home a few minutes ago. A slow day in the law business. Sit down, March. May I offer you a drink?"

"Why not?" I said. "I'll have some bourbon with soda or water on the side."

He nodded and stepped behind a small bar. He poured the

bourbon—and I noticed that he used a heavy hand—and the soda, and brought them over to me. He looked at his wife. "My dear?"

"Perhaps a little sherry," she said.

He poured that and served it to her. Then he mixed a scotch and soda for himself and came over to sit next to me. "I understand you are a representative of Intercontinental Insurance."

"That is correct, sir," I said.

"I hope you'll pardon me, but do you have identification?"

I nodded and fished out my ID card. He looked at it carefully and handed it back. "I presume that you are here in reference to our claim concerning the recent robbery?"

"Yes."

"I don't think I understand," he said. "I had our accountant make out the forms. Was there an error in them?"

"No errors," I said with a smile. "This is merely a routine visit. It is customary whenever there is a large amount of money involved. I hope you don't mind?"

"Not at all, not at all. Go right ahead, March."

"Thank you," I said dryly. "First, I noticed something rather unusual in your policy. About half of your jewels were unset diamonds. That is rather unusual. It has nothing to do with your claim, but I am curious."

"It's very simple," he said. "They were bought as a form of investment. I will frankly admit that I am not too happy about certain political trends in our country, and I have taken to investing in diamonds as a hedge against possible inflation."

"Very astute of you," I agreed. "I understand that with the

exception of special occasions, most of your jewelry was kept in boxes in the Palm National Bank in Beverly Hills."

"That is correct."

"Mrs. Carleton's jewelry would naturally be taken out and kept here when she was expecting to wear them. But why were the unset diamonds removed to the house at that particular time?"

"There was a man coming that particular weekend who was a potential buyer of the loose diamonds. I had asked a price which would have allowed me a very generous profit, so I was anxious to show them to him. They were removed from the bank for that reason. I might point out that this was perfectly consistent with our insurance policy."

"I'm aware of that," I said. "I was just curious. I gather that you never had the opportunity of showing them to the potential buyer?"

"Unfortunately, no."

"Do you recall where you were the night of the robbery?"

"All too well," he said. "We had dinner at the Suckling Pig and then went to the theater."

"And you arrived home at what time?"

"Perhaps one o'clock. We stopped off for a bite before coming home."

"Where were the servants that night?"

"We had given them the evening off. Except for the gardener, who has an apartment over the garage. He was apparently asleep and heard nothing. But surely, March, you could get all of this from the police."

"I could, but I prefer not to do so. It is too easy to fall into the trap of accepting what the police say, whereas the owners might have more insight."

"I see. Very intelligent of you, March."

"Thank you," I said politely. "Where was the jewelry kept when you had it in the house?"

"In our wall safe. As a matter of fact, in this room." He walked over to the wall and moved a picture to one side to reveal a safe door. "It was supposed to be one of the best you can buy. But someone broke into it."

I nodded. "Obviously. Mr. Carleton, do you know of a man named Johnny Renaldi?"

"You mean the man who was murdered the other night? I didn't know him, but since I am a criminal lawyer I had heard of him. I also know that the police had suspected him of being part of the robbery gang."

I looked at Mrs. Carleton. "I couldn't help noticing how lovely your house is as the maid showed me in. Who decorated it?"

"Lita Harper. She did such a lovely job. I was shocked that the police thought she had something to do with the murder of that man. I thought she was a lady."

"If you ask me," her husband said, "she was probably working with him."

"Oh, no," she exclaimed, "I can't believe it. She was such a lovely girl."

"I didn't ask for that reason," I said. "I was merely asking because I admired the way the house is decorated. I hope you understand that this is not an investigation. We like to meet the policyholders in such situations and talk to them just in case they remember something which might be important. We don't mind paying on a claim, but we still like to recover the property and to discourage other people from robbing our clients."

"Very understandable," Carleton said. "Sorry we couldn't be of more help."

"You've helped," I said, without knowing what I meant. "Thank you for seeing me."

"We're always glad to assist," he boomed. He got up and stood there while I thanked his wife, then he accompanied me to the front door. "Glad you came to see us, March," he said, patting me on the back in a way that helped me to take the two steps through the door. "We'll wait to hear from you," he added, just before he closed the door.

I got into my car and checked the next address and my Beverly Hills street map. The next place was that of the William Grants. I drove to it. The house and the grounds were about the same as the Carletons's. So was the maid who answered the door and then escorted me through the house to a study.

Mr. Grant, a stockbroker, wasn't at home, but his wife greeted me with warmth and a bourbon with chaser. The story was pretty much the same. They normally kept their jewels in the Palm National Bank but had taken them out for the weekend because they intended to go to a ballet performance. The night of the robbery they had gone to the Suckling Pig for dinner, then had spent the evening at a friend's house. Lita Harper had decorated their house, and they were very fond of her. They had never heard of Johnny Renaldi. Their jewelry was insured for $500,000.

Mr. and Mrs. Herman Baines were next. Mr. Baines wasn't home either, and Mrs. Baines obviously had a very low opinion of insurance persons. She had lost jewelry insured for $350,000, and the only thing she wanted to know was when she would get the money. She didn't even offer me a cup of tea. She grudgingly admitted that Lita Harper had decorated her house and indignantly denied that it was possible for her and her husband to know such a person as Johnny Renaldi. She didn't think it was any of my business, but did admit that they had gone to the Suckling Pig for dinner the night of the robbery and that her jewelry was normally kept at the Palm National Bank.

The home of Mr. and Mrs. Thomas Ray wasn't quite as fancy as the others, but it was still worth a lot of blue chip stamps. They were also younger, but they already had the Beverly Hills mark on them. Mr. Ray was home. He was in real estate and he'd been showing someone a house in the neighborhood and decided not to go back to the office. He wanted to give me a scotch, but finally managed to produce a bourbon.

"It's not the money, you understand," he explained. They had $250,000 coming. "We'd much rather get the jewelry back. There were pieces that have a sentimental value: anniversary presents, birthday presents, things like that, you know. Right, baby?"

"Right, hon," she said.

I took a swallow of bourbon to ease my stomach. "I understand," I said. I did, too. I could get very sentimental about $250,000. "How come you took the jewelry out of the bank that weekend?"

"We were going to a bash on Saturday night. Some charity

thing at the Hollywood Bowl. Baby's great on charity things. So we took them out to pretty her up."

"Who knew that you took them out?"

"Well, I guess the bank did."

"That's the Palm National Bank?"

"Right."

"What about your servants?"

"Well, I don't think they knew the sparklers were in the house. Right, baby?"

"I don't think they knew, hon," she said. "I put them in the safe the minute I got home that day. I remember that Mildred was busy in the kitchen and Yvonne was cleaning upstairs."

"That was a Friday?" I asked.

"Yes."

"You went out Friday night?"

"Yes."

"Where?"

"We had dinner at the Suckling Pig and then went to a movie. After the movie we stopped in at a place on the Strip and had a few drinks. We got home about two."

"That was the night of the robbery?"

"Yes."

"Were the servants in the house?"

"No. Both of them had the night off."

"When did you discover that you had been robbed?"

"Almost as soon as we were in the house," he said. "I came in here and saw the safe door open. I called the police at once. They discovered that someone had broken a window in the back to get into the house."

"Anything else stolen?"

"Just the jewelry. I guess they knew what they wanted."

"Did you ever meet Johnny Renaldi?"

"The guy who was killed the other night? No. I think I saw him in a restaurant one night a couple of months ago. Somebody pointed him out and said he was a gangster. But that's all."

"Did you go to the Suckling Pig often?"

"Once or twice a week, I guess."

I finished the bourbon and put the glass down. He didn't offer to replenish it. "Lita Harper decorated your house?"

"Oh, yes," Mrs. Ray said. "She did a wonderful job too. I was so shocked to read that they think she killed that gangster. I just can't believe it."

"Hey, I remember now," he said. "She was with him that night somebody pointed him out to me. That's probably the story. She got a bad case of hot pants and so she helped him line up his robberies."

"Oh, hon," his wife said.

"Well, it's probably true, baby," he answered. "You know that things like that happen. Everyone didn't have the sort of sheltered upbringing you did."

"Well, thanks," I said. "We'll be in touch with you."

"Sure," he said. He got up and walked to the front door with me. "Maybe I was a little rough in my language," he said before I left. "The little woman isn't used to language like that, but that's the way life is. You know how it is, Mr. March."

"Sure, hon," I said, and walked out. The door slammed loudly behind me as I got into the car.

Miss Pamela Perry lived in a small but attractive house up in the hills. The records said that she was an agent, single, and had lost jewelry insured for $200,000. She turned out to be a very attractive brunette, about thirty-five. She took one look at me and offered me a martini. I took one look at her and accepted.

"Where's my money?" she asked when she brought the drink.

"In the bank," I said. "Intercontinental takes a dim view of letting money just float around, especially if their investigators are available."

She laughed. "So they sent you around to talk me into forgetting the whole thing?"

"Not at all. I'm here because we don't like people to steal from our policyholders. We prefer to discourage such activities."

"I'm all for that. But I don't see what I can do to help. I've already told the police all that I know."

"Bear with me a minute," I said, "at least until I finish this martini. Did you know Johnny Renaldi?"

"I met him once at a restaurant. Lita Harper introduced him to me, but that was all."

"Miss Harper decorated your house?"

"Yes. Lovely, isn't it?"

"Very nice. Are you and Miss Harper friends?"

"Not exactly. I've known her for some time, and we've often been to the same parties. We're not really friends, but I like her and I don't think that she had anything to do with the robberies or that she killed that crumb."

"You mean Renaldi?"

"Sure. He was a crumb. Are you trying to tell me that you agree with the cops and think she's guilty?"

"No. I was there when the murder was discovered, and I'm certain that she didn't do it. I saw her this morning and told her that I would help her as much as I could. But let's get back to you. You normally kept your jewelry in the Palm National Bank, didn't you?"

"Yes."

"Why did you remove it that weekend?"

"I was invited to the home of a client in Palm Springs, and there was a fairly fancy party planned for Saturday night. I planned to be all decked out. It's part of the business."

"The robbery was on Friday night?"

She nodded. "I was supposed to leave Saturday morning for Palm Springs. Instead, I was here with a houseful of cops."

"But you were out Friday night?"

"Yes. I went to dinner and a play with a friend. We did a little pub crawling later, and he brought me home sometime between one and two in the morning."

"When did you discover that you had been robbed?"

"Not until the next morning. I was tired when I got home that night and went right to sleep without looking through the house."

"Any servants at home?"

"Not that night. I have a sleep-in maid, but since I was going away I gave her the weekend off, and she left Friday afternoon to visit her parents in Nevada."

"She's still with you?"

She smiled. "Yes. And you'll find that the police checked her out very thoroughly."

"Okay," I said. "I don't suppose you just happened to have dinner that Friday night at the Suckling Pig, did you?"

"As a matter of fact, we did. Of course, I go there quite often—but how did you guess?"

"Sheer talent," I said.

I finished my martini and left. She walked to the front door with me and suggested that I keep in touch with her about the case.

"I might even have better answers the next time," she said lightly.

"Maybe I should have better questions," I suggested. "I'll be in touch with you." I gave her a last appreciative look and went out to my car.

The last one on the list was Kitty Mills. I knew she was a fairly successful supporting actress in pictures. I remembered seeing her in a number of films. She lived in a small house surrounded by trees, equipped with a swimming pool and even a babbling brook.

A maid answered the door and told me that Miss Mills was not at home but was expected back in about two hours. I left word that I would check back with her.

I headed south down the hill, thinking I'd drop in for another visit with the police. I'd driven no more than two blocks when I became aware that I was being followed again. It wasn't the same black car this time, but my guess was that it was the same driver. He stuck pretty close to me without showing signs of trying to cut around me. If he wanted to follow me to the police station, that was all right with me, so I relaxed.

The street curved around the hill down to where it connected with Laurel Canyon Boulevard. I reached it, intending to make a left turn, but then I saw something that made me hesitate. There was a car parked sideways in the middle of the boulevard. I didn't know if its presence had anything to do with me, but I didn't feel like finding out the hard way. I swung my car to the right and headed the opposite way on Laurel Canyon.

Driving at a moderate speed, I kept glancing in my rearview mirror. The car that had been following turned the corner and fell in behind me, staying at about the same distance. Then I saw the parked car straighten out and drive after us. It was moving faster than we were, and looked as if it might be intending to pass us. *Well, March,* I said to myself, *this may be the hour of truth for somebody.*

Laurel Canyon is hardly the ideal place for a drag race. It is a winding road with frequent sharp curves. While there wasn't much traffic at the moment, I didn't feel like seeing how fast I could whip the Cadillac around the curves. Driving with one hand, I reached inside my coat and pulled my gun from the holster. I held it in my lap and kept checking on the second car.

It was a fairly recent compact and it was moving fast as it passed the car behind me. The driver was the only person in it. There was a straight stretch of road ahead of us, and he was obviously going to take advantage of it. If he was after me, he might do one of two things. He could attack me as our two cars drew even with each other, or he might cut quickly in front of me, trying to force me off the road or maybe just bring me to a stop. It was unlikely that he would try to crash into me. The Cadillac was too heavy for that sort of move.

My side mirror showed him drawing up on my left. I waited until he was almost even, then glanced over at him, ready to bring my gun up. He was not anyone I recognized. He didn't even look at me, and seemed intent only on his driving. Then he was moving ahead of me.

I slackened speed and got both hands on the steering wheel. Again he fooled me. He didn't cut sharply in front of me, but remained on the left until he was a safe distance ahead and then swung gradually into the right lane. A moment later he disappeared from sight around the next curve.

Feeling a little foolish, I put my gun away. There was always a chance, however, that he planned on getting ahead of me and then blocking the road so that I would be sandwiched between the two cars. That seemed to be a wrong guess, too, for each time I'd spot him, he'd be farther and farther ahead of me.

Finally I forgot about him and turned my attention to more immediate things. The car behind me was still there. I could have turned around and gone back the way I'd originally intended, but it would have meant turning into a private driveway, and I decided against it. If Polerri—and I was sure he was my shadow—had any idea of catching me off guard, that might give him a good chance. There wasn't far to go until Laurel Canyon would come down out of the hills and cross Ventura Boulevard in the Valley.

I topped the hill and the panoramic view of Studio City was spread out before me. I rounded the next curve and forgot the view below as I discovered I had been right in the first place. The compact car was parked right across the road without quite enough room to go around either end. The driver was out of the car, standing at the edge of the road with a gun in his hand and a smile on his face.

SIX

There wasn't much choice, and less time in which to make one. I could crash into the parked car and hope I survived. I could stop and either lift up my hands or try to shoot it out. I could also aim the car at the man standing on the road, close my eyes, and hope that I'd take him with me as I hurtled straight down the side of the mountain.

I did the only thing I could think of under the circumstances. I stepped on the accelerator as hard as I could, swung as far left as possible, then straightened out as the Cadillac leaped forward. I caught the front of the compact car with a screeching protest of metal. The Cadillac seemed to hesitate for a second, then surged forward again, tossing the smaller car away from it the way a big dog might throw a rat. I was struggling to keep the Cadillac from careening into the bank on my left, but out of the corner of my eye I saw the compact rolling toward the drop on the right.

Back in the center of the road again, I started braking for a sharp turn as the road dipped down the hill. I made it with protesting tires. I risked a brief glance over my right shoulder. The compact car was just tumbling off the road.

The other car had stopped to pick up the man on the road. I turned my attention back to my driving and pushed the Cadillac as fast as I dared. At the cost of some more rubber from the tires, I made it to Ventura Boulevard without spotting the other car in my rearview mirror. I had a bit of luck. I got through a green light just before it changed. Then it was only a short distance to the freeway. I pushed the car up to sixty-five and held it there until I reached the Sunset exit.

I drove a few blocks up Sunset and stopped to look at the Cadillac. It had come through the encounter in pretty good shape. There was some damage to the front bumper and part of the grille, but not too much. A few small scratches on the left side were left from brushing the hill, but that was all. I got back in and drove out to see the Beverly Hills police.

"Maybe I should fix up an office for you," Lieutenant O'Brien said sourly as I entered his office. "Or does this mean that you have solved the case for me?"

"Not quite," I said with a smile. "I thought you might be sitting here waiting to cooperate with me, so I rushed right over."

"How the hell can I cooperate when you don't give me time to do any work?"

"Oh, come now, Lieutenant. You've had all day."

"Very funny. I suppose you've been working?"

"All day."

"Doing what?"

"Legwork. Covering a lot of ground that you people must have covered already, but you didn't offer me any cooperation on the results. I went first this morning to see Lita Harper. Then I went around to see the robbery victims who were insured by my company. All but one, and I'll see her later."

"So, what did you learn?" he growled. "The Harper dame

claims she's innocent. They all do. And all you learned from the other people was that they and their servants were out the nights of the robberies, that they all knew the Harper dame, and none of them knew Johnny Renaldi. And you can get something else from Lieutenant Cooper. He followed up all of those stories, including the servants, and everything checked out. The only leak was through Lita Harper, and she's the only one who knew Renaldi. And the only one of that group to shack up with him. He'll give you your cooperation."

"Okay," I said, "how about Danny Polerri?"

"We've checked on him and still are. There is nothing to tie him with the robberies except that he knew Renaldi. And he has an alibi for the time that Renaldi was killed."

"He probably finds it easy to rig an alibi."

"Not this one," he said. "Five minutes before Renaldi was killed, he was getting a ticket for running through a red light. And he was at least thirty minutes away from Renaldi's apartment."

"Great. How's his alibi for today?"

That startled him. "What do you mean?"

"When I left the county jail this morning, I was followed by Danny Polerri. After I made a stop at the Intercontinental office, I caught him waiting for me. I got the drop on him and give him the bum's rush. But somehow he picked me up again this afternoon. He was driving a different car, but I'm sure it was Polerri. Incidentally, do you know a friend of his who's about five eleven, weighs about one-ninety, has a thin mustache, dark hair, and, I think, a gold or silver tooth in front?"

"Sounds like George Lotti. He's a friend of Polerri's and has a record. Why?"

I told him what had happened. For the first time, he was looking interested. "Where did you say this happened?" he asked when I'd finished.

"At the top of the hill on Laurel Canyon, just before you start down on the way to Ventura Boulevard."

"What kind of a car?"

"Dodge Dart. Black. Sorry, but I was too busy to get the license number."

"Maybe we can find out something about it," he said. He pulled a phone over and dialed a number. "Lieutenant Black," he said after a moment. Again he waited. "Hello, Pete," he said then. "This is Nathan O'Brien in Beverly Hills. How have you been?" He listened, then answered. "Fine. You know how it is with all of us cops. Our feet hurt, we're overworked, and the taxpayers get mad at us because we don't do more, while our wives are mad at us because we do so much. Incidentally, Pete, I wanted to ask about an accident that happened out in your area about an hour ago, on Laurel Canyon up on top of the hill. A black Dodge Dart."

This time he listened for several minutes, occasionally making a noise to indicate he was paying attention.

"Sounds like quite a story, Pete. We might have something to help. I'll let you know after I've checked it out. Thanks for telling me about it. And let's get together if we ever get a day off." He hung up and swung around to face me.

"They found the car, all right. It was pretty well smashed up. Nobody around and nobody who saw the accident happen. They checked the registration and found it belonged to George Lotti of Hollywood. They got in touch with the Hollywood police and discovered that Lotti had reported his car stolen. The report was by phone and it was made about thirty minutes after the accident."

"Pretty," I said. "By this time he'll have himself a good alibi covering the time, and it'll be my word against his that he was there at all."

"He could play it another way," the Lieutenant said slowly. "He could change his story and admit he was there. He could say his car broke down and that he tried to flag the first car that came along. That was you. Instead of stopping, he will say, you tried to run him down. He jumped out of the way in time, but you smashed into his car and then drove away as fast as you could. He caught a ride with the next car to come along."

"And the report that his car was stolen?"

"Simple. He'll merely say that you were trying to kill him and that he was frightened enough to lie at first. Can you swear that it was Danny Polerri who was following you and who picked up Lotti?"

I shook my head. "I'm sure of it, but I can't swear to it."

"Legally, your position," he said, "is not too good. You can't prove that you were followed, and you can't prove that Lotti deliberately blocked your way and was threatening you with a gun. On the other hand, if he wishes, he can probably prove that you smashed into his car and left the scene of an accident. An examination of your car would certainly prove the contact, and you made no effort to report the accident to the local police."

I stared at him. "I have a feeling you're trying to tell me something, Lieutenant."

"Not at all," he said innocently. "I am merely having a private conversation with a man who is cooperating with me on another matter. And I might add a bit of information that you will find interesting in support of your theory. One thing bothered me as you first told your story. It would be difficult for two men in different cars to work together without some sort of fast communication. Even then, the timing might be difficult. I think I know the answer now."

"What?"

"Lieutenant Black made two interesting discoveries in the wrecked car. He found transistor sending and receiving sets. They were probably powerful enough for operation at the distances they traveled. But there was an even more interesting gadget in the car."

"Don't tell me," I groaned, "let me guess. They were tracking me electronically. I should have thought of that, but I guess I didn't think they'd be smart enough to be so modern."

"We have very progressive hoods in California," he said dryly. "If I were you, I'd look over your car. I'll bet there's a beep box fastened to it somewhere. Am I being cooperative enough?"

"You're doing fine, Lieutenant. Now what do we do about Lotti?"

"It's out of my jurisdiction."

"Meaning that we do nothing?"

"I'm not saying anything like that," he said mildly. "In fact, I don't recall discussing anything with you that has happened outside of Beverly Hills."

"You think I'd just butt my head against a wall?"

"Well, won't you?"

"Probably. But I don't like to forget things."

"You say you're a pusher. So do a little pushing until you have something on them, something that will stick. There is something you might keep in mind."

"What?"

"Polerri and Lotti never earned an honest dollar in their lives. Any cop out here would be glad to put them away. It is even possible that they were involved in the jewel robberies, but get it through your head that neither the robberies nor the murder of Renaldi have anything to do with the fact that Polerri is so hot for you."

"How can you be so sure of that? He told me not to try to get Lita Harper off the hook. And what other reason could he have? I've never seen him before."

"But you have."

"Where?"

"I've been doing a little checking on both of you. Polerri wasn't very important when you saw him, and you probably don't remember him. He has what he thinks are two good reasons for remembering you, and he's made threats about getting you for them."

"What are they?"

"A few years ago you came out to Los Angeles on an arson case. Remember it?"*

I nodded. "What does that have to do with it?"

"You nailed several people on that case, but among them

---

* See *Softly in the Night* by M.E. Chaber.

was a big shot from New York named Harry Manfred, and the torch who was a dame named Lillian Cassidy. Danny Polerri was brought here as one of Manfred's boys, and he also had a big yen for the Cassidy girl. He wants to even things up for them."

"His loyalty is touching," I said. "Okay, I'll remember it. Anything else?"

"How the hell can I have anything else when I spend all my time getting you straightened out? Now go away. Go find somebody else to bother."

"If you keep on being so friendly," I told him, "you'll get me kicked out of the private detective's union. I'll see you soon, Lieutenant."

"Not too soon—I hope."

I gave him my best smile and left. Then I took his advice about bothering someone else. I went across to the office of Lieutenant Cooper. The big detective looked up as I entered and waved me to a chair.

"Find some jewelry?" he asked.

"A pair of cuff links in my coat pocket. Does that help?"

"About as much as anyone else has turned up. These boys must either be loaded or they have discovered a secret outlet. The first robbery was almost six months ago, and so far we haven't found a single piece of missing jewelry. Usually it starts turning up pretty quickly. That doesn't mean that the case is always solved that soon, but we do start finding a piece here and there. This time, nothing. I was just sitting here brooding about it."

"That reminds me of something I wanted to ask you. How

many cases are there which you think were pulled by the same gang?"

"You don't know?"

"I know about the six cases which we had insured. I don't know about the others."

"Well, there are fifteen cases which we are pretty certain were the work of the same gang. There might be some others we're missing."

"Sounds like a tidy sum of money."

"The value is about six million dollars, but even if they fence all of it, they ought to get more than a million. I doubt if they could fence that much out here. They might spread it around over the country, but some of it should be showing up."

"How many do you think are in the gang?"

"Probably seven or eight—including Miss Harper and Renaldi."

"What about Danny Polerri, George Lotti, Mack Larry, and Little Benjy Macklin?"

He frowned. "Not Macklin, I think. He's nothing but a strong-arm man. The other three are good possibilities. They were all three friends of Renaldi and have been known to work with him. Another interesting thing is that they have all been supplied with money for the past six months, although they haven't been suspected of pulling any jobs."

"And since no jewelry has shown up, it indicates that some-one is paying them a salary to wait for the eventual split?"

"That's my guess."

"Then somebody has been running the whole show. Who? Renaldi?"

"I don't think so. I don't think he was smart enough or had enough money. My guess is he was like a second in command. It has occasionally occurred to me that Miss Harper is a likely candidate."

"Tell me something else," I said. "Did all of the victims normally keep their jewelry at the Palm National Bank?"

He smiled. "All of them."

"And was each victim having dinner at the Suckling Pig the night he or she was robbed?"

"Yes. Interesting, isn't it?"

"I imagine that you've checked on it?"

He nodded. "Again and again—and we'll keep it up. I'm certain that someone in the restaurant passed the word when intended victims dined there, and that someone in the bank did the same thing when jewelry was taken out. In the first place, it could be anyone from the restaurant owner down to the busboys. We haven't found any contact yet. There are only five possible suspects in the bank. We've checked every damn inch of their lives without finding a thing. So there's nothing to do but keep at it until we find what we have been missing."

"Somebody had to be the custodian of the jewelry. Got any ideas on that?"

"Lots of them. One of our favorite candidates was Renaldi. Yesterday I had high hopes that we would find the jewels— but we didn't."

"Why yesterday?"

"Well, we had searched the apartment where he was killed, without any luck. Then, yesterday, the Los Angeles police discovered that Renaldi had a second apartment in Hollywood. I went there with them. We went over it with everything, including a vacuum cleaner, but didn't find anything. There were only two personal items in the place: a bottle of whiskey in the refrigerator and a carton of cigarettes."

"The vacuum cleaner pick up anything?"

"Sure, a lot of dirt and cigarette ashes, some dandruff from the bed, and hairs—blond, brunette, red. It was obviously a place where he took women when he didn't want to spend too much time with them and didn't want them to know where he lived."

"A list of the girls?"

"No. It would have taken the whole police force to keep track of Renaldi's girls, especially the one-night stands. It was enough to keep up with the steadier ones like Miss Harper."

"Did he have many steady ones?"

"She was the only one we know of during the past seven months."

"How long had he been living in the apartment where he was killed?"

"Eight months. Before that he lived in a more modest apartment a little north of the Silver Lake area of Los Angeles. He gave it up when he moved to Beverly Hills."

"Do you suppose I could take a look at the apartment where he was killed and the one he kept in Hollywood?"

"It's all right with me. All of his things are still in the Beverly Hills place, and except for the tramping around we did, it's still the same as when we pulled his body out. His rent was paid up for another month and nobody has claimed his possessions yet. The other place might represent a small problem. His rent was due today there, and after we covered everything we gave the owner permission to rent it. If you can find anything we missed, you're welcome to it."

"Thanks," I said. I stood up. "One more thing, Lieutenant. Did Lita Harper decorate the homes of all the victims?"

"No," he admitted. "She did decorate the homes of all but three of them. Of the three, she was in two of the houses to give an estimate. And she had been in the third home on social occasions."

"Thanks for nothing," I muttered.

"You're welcome." He laughed. "But you're forgetting one thing, son. Where's your half of the cooperation?"

"I haven't come to it yet," I said. "I've been spending my time talking to victims and the rest of it ducking Danny Polerri's attempts to clobber me. I'll be glad to cooperate by letting you be the target half of the time. In the meantime, you can do one more thing for me."

"What?"

"Give me the address of Renaldi's Hollywood apartment. And if you have it, you can give me the address of his old place."

He looked at me narrowly. "What do you want that one for?"

"I don't know," I admitted. "I might get a lead on some of his girlfriends. And I might just waste my time."

He pulled out a sheet of paper and scribbled on it. He handed it to me. "The first one is the Hollywood apartment. I'll expect a report."

"Naturally," I said. I closed the door behind me before he could answer.

I went out to the Cadillac and made a thorough search of it. Finally I found the beep box underneath the body, a handy little device that would broadcast a beep every few seconds, to be picked up by a receiver in another car. With the aid of it, someone could follow me without being seen and find me easily, if he wasn't too far away. I removed it and put it on the front seat. It would still broadcast until I wanted to get rid of it. I got in and drove off, going to Sunset and then turning in the direction of Los Angeles. I checked the rearview mirror, but didn't spot a car that looked suspicious.

I drove several blocks and turned to the right. I made two or three more turns before I threw the beep box out of the window. I stepped up my speed and made a number of other turns, hit Melrose Avenue, and drove for about ten blocks before I cut back to Santa Monica Boulevard. I stopped at the nearest bar-and-grill that had parking space in the rear. I went in and ordered a drink. Halfway through it, I went to the phone booth and dialed the number of Kitty Mills. The maid answered the phone.

"This is Mr. March of Intercontinental Insurance," I told her. "I was there earlier this afternoon. Is Miss Mills home yet?"

"Just a moment," she said.

A little later, there was another voice on the phone. "Hello," she said.

"Hello," I answered. "This is Milo March. I represent Intercontinental Insurance. It's about your jewelry."

I know," she said. Her voice had a delightful singing quality. "Doreen told me that you were here earlier. What can I do for you, Mr. March?"

"I'd like to talk to you about the loss of your jewelry. Tonight, if possible."

"I don't know about tonight. I was planning to stay home in a pair of slacks and a sweatshirt—which means no visitors—having a sandwich and a glass of milk and then reading a script."

"I'll compromise with you," I told her. "I'll take you out to dinner and we can talk business. Then I'll drive you home and you can read the script."

There was a short pause. "You drive a hard bargain, Mr. March," she said. "I suppose I must talk to you. All right. Pick me up in two hours and I will have dinner with you. But I must be right back after to read the script."

"It's a deal. Where would you like to have dinner? The Suckling Pig?"

"Oh, you know it?" she said. She sounded delighted. "That would be fine. I'll see you then." She hung up.

I replaced the receiver and went back to my drink. I strolled outside and checked. I couldn't spot anyone, so I got in the car and headed for Hollywood. I still watched, but didn't see anyone following me.

The address of Renaldi's second apartment was on Carlton Way. I discovered it was between Hollywood and Sunset boulevards and just off Wilton Place. It turned out to be a nest of bungalow apartments. His had been number eight. I parked and walked into the court to look at it. There was already an empty look about it.

I was still standing there when a young man, about seventeen, came out of a nearby bungalow. He looked at me curiously.

"There ain't nobody living there now, mister," he said.

"Oh?" I said. "I was wondering if it was empty. The other tenant moved away, huh?"

"You could call it that. I heard somebody like killed him. The fuzz was here yesterday."

"Was he killed here?"

"Nah. He wasn't here much. He was a swinger. He only showed up here when he had some chick in tow."

"Had a lot of girls, huh?"

"I'll say. He was bringing one here at least once a week for a long time. A blonde. Strictly from Stacksville, if you dig me."

"I dig you the most," I said solemnly. "You don't suppose any of that rubbed off on the apartment, do you?"

"You looking for a pad?" he asked.

"I had something of the sort in mind. Someone told me that there was a vacant apartment here, and I was just wondering if this was it."

"It's empty, all right. The old biddy who rents it is in apartment two. Say, you got any of those blondes from Stacksville?"

"I've known a few."

"I dig them, dad. You round up any spares, just whistle for me, okay?"

"I'll do that," I said gravely. I watched him as he walked away, then went to apartment two and knocked.

He'd been right. She was an old biddy.

She opened the door and peered at me. "I don't want to buy anything," she said.

"I have nothing to sell," I told her. "I'm interested in renting an apartment. I believe you have one that is vacant. Number eight?"

"How'd you know?"

"I've been looking around the neighborhood for an apartment, and a young man who lives here told me that number eight was vacant."

"Well, it is. It's all cleaned up, but we ain't put up a sign yet. It's ninety dollars a month, furnished. Utilities are included. One month in advance. You want to see it?"

"If I may."

"I'll get the key."

She was back in a moment with a passkey and led the way to the bungalow. She unlocked the door and threw it open. I went in and made a pretense of looking at it. Except for one thing, it looked like dozens of other furnished apartments. The furniture was adequate but dreary-looking. The rooms weren't large, and the kitchen was especially small, as though the owner felt that anyone who took it would be doing very little cooking. The exceptional thing was that the bedroom and living room, from the floor halfway up to the ceiling, was paneled in fine-looking wood. The rest of the walls and the ceiling were wallpapered, and the paper was stained and faded. The ceiling was the worst, buckling and bulging in spots as though the rains had come through a number of times.

"It looks fine," I said. "I'll take it."

"How many of you?" she asked.

"Just me."

"I hope you ain't like the last tenant."

"Not knowing what he was like, I can hardly answer."

"He was a wencher," she said through tight lips, "always bringing some hussy around. And up to no good, you can count on it."

"I daresay," I said. "I'm afraid I'm not the same sort. I work much too hard for such things."

"Pay me the money and I'll give you the key."

I counted out ninety dollars and she handed over the key. "What kind of work do you do, young man?"

"I work in insurance."

"A good, steady job. I'll make out the receipt and leave it in your mailbox. What name?"

"John Milo," I said.

She nodded and we both left the apartment. I made sure that the door was locked and went out to my car. I wasn't far from my favorite Hollywood bar and I still had some time to kill. I drove over to it and went in. I ordered a drink, then went to the phone and called the Suckling Pig. I made a reservation in the name of Milo March and went back to my drink.

Big Joe wasn't around, so I drank slowly and talked idly with the bartender when he wasn't busy. When enough time had slipped by, I went out and drove to Beverly Hills. I parked in front of Kitty Mills's house and went up and rang the bell. The door was opened by the same maid.

"Come in, Mr. March," she said. "Miss Mills is ready."

She came down the stairs just as I entered. I had to admit that she looked even more lovely in person than on the screen. I told her so as she came up to me.

"Thank you, Mr. March," she said, giving me her hand. "I didn't know insurance men were so gallant."

"I couldn't tell you," I admitted. "I never associate with them."

She laughed and the maid arrived with her mink stole. She threw it around her shoulders. "I'll be home early, Doreen, but you needn't wait up. Shall we go, Mr. March?"

"Why not?" I said.

We went out to the car. I helped her into the front seat and walked around and slid under the wheel. I swung around and headed back the way I had come.

"I haven't known many insurance men," she said, "except the ones who have sold me policies, but I don't think I have known any who drove new Cadillacs. You must be at least a vice-president, Mr. March."

"Call me Milo and I'll tell you the secret."

She laughed. "All right, Milo."

"Expense account," I said.

"I don't understand."

"Strictly speaking, I'm not even an employee of Intercontinental."

She looked startled, then frightened. "Are—are you trying to tell me that I'm being kidnapped—or something like that?"

It was my turn to laugh. "Nothing like that. I do work for Intercontinental, but I am not an employee. I guess you might call me a contract worker. When they have a special job, they call me in and I take it—for a price plus expenses. In between, I work for other companies in the same way."

"That wasn't fair. You were deliberately trying to frighten me. But what does it have to do with the car?"

"Everything. I live in New York City. I have offices on Madison Avenue not far from the offices of the various companies for whom I work. I am an insurance investigator. When I don't work, I travel from my apartment to my office, a very comfortable taxi ride. When I do work, I travel by planes, boats, or rented cars—all of which go on the expense account. Therefore, I see no reason why I shouldn't travel the way I like to. I eat and drink on about the same level whether I'm working or not. And there's the story of my life."

She laughed again. "At last, a truthful man. Do you know why I agreed to have dinner with you, Milo?"

"Couldn't resist me?" I asked hopefully.

"I couldn't resist what Doreen said about you. She usually disapproves of the men I go out with. But in your case she predicted that if I said I was just going to stay home, you would invite me to dinner and she said I must go. It made me curious."

"As long as it worked," I said.

I was checking the street signs as we drove along and finally realized we were nearing the restaurant. "Kitty," I said, "would you play along with a slight bit of eccentricity on my part?"

"Sure. What?"

"Honey, you should always ask what before you say sure. I'm going to stop and park near the first taxi stand we see and we're going to take a taxi the rest of the way."

"But why?"

"I told you I was eccentric. I don't like to be too conspicuous."

"And you drive a white Cadillac? All right, Milo."

I spotted a taxi stand and found a parking space. We got into a cab and drove the rest of the way to the restaurant. We were greeted royally by the maître d', who not only remembered that I had a reservation but was delighted to see my companion.

"Thank you, Emile," she said. "I hope that you gave Mr. March a good table."

"The best, Miss Mills," he said. "Emile has been taking reservations too long to make such a mistake. This way, please."

He led us through the plush restaurant to a table which was undoubtedly one of the best. A waiter was there as soon as we were seated. We both ordered dry martinis. When they came, they were also the best.

"The best for the best," I told her, lifting my glass.

"You see," she said, responding, "you not only have a way with maids but with people like Emile. I never knew him to do so well by a stranger before."

I was a little curious about that myself, but I didn't mention it. "It's just my natural charm," I said. "I hope that it registers as well with fine young actresses."

"I thank you, sir, for both the fine and the young, but not for the plural. Now, what is this business you wanted to discuss?"

I groaned. "Must I?"

"You must. You lured me out for that purpose, so you must go through with it."

I fortified myself with another sip of the martini. "All right. You were robbed on a Friday night, right?"

"Yes."

"And you took your jewelry out of the bank that day?"

"Yes."

"Why?"

"I was going to a special party on Saturday night thrown by my newest producer. It was a glitter party."

"And you had dinner here that Friday night?"

"Yes."

"With whom?"

She smiled at me. "I don't think the insurance company is unduly concerned about that. Just say with a friend."

"All right. Where was your maid that night?"

"She had a date and got home later than I did. She has already been completely cleared by the police."

"Did Lita Harper decorate your apartment?"

"Yes. And if you're asking that because of those terrible newspaper stories about her, then I think you're horrid."

"I'm not asking for that reason. If it makes you feel better, I don't think she's guilty of murder—although at the moment I'm about the only one who doesn't. Did you know Johnny Renaldi?"

"I knew him by sight, but I was never introduced to him and never talked to him."

"Okay, honey. The business hour is over."

"That's all there is to it? You don't want to ask me all sorts of questions about my debts, do I play the horses, and am I supporting a man who's a wastrel, as they always do in my movies?"

"Not me. I know an honest face when I see one."

"I didn't know you'd noticed."

"We detectives are trained to observe everything," I said gravely, "including the fact that your glass is empty."

We had two more martinis and then ordered dinner. It, too, was excellent. After dinner we ordered brandy and coffee. While it was being brought, I excused myself and went back toward the men's room. It was at the rear of the building, beyond the kitchen. As I had hoped, there was also an exit near it. I pushed it open slightly and saw that it led out to the parking lot. The area next to the building was in shadow, so I stepped outside.

There were perhaps twenty cars in the parking lot. At first I could see nothing but the lines of empty cars, but a moment later I caught a movement in one of them. I concentrated on it. Then someone in the car lit a cigarette, carefully shielding the blaze. It wasn't enough to show any detail, but I could tell that there were at least two persons sitting in the car.

I slipped into the club again and went back to the table. The coffee and brandy were already there. I tasted the brandy. It was good.

"Fate cannot harm me," I said, hoping it was true. "I have dined tonight—and met a beautiful woman."

"For a minute I was afraid I'd been replaced by a snifter of brandy."

"I don't think you have to worry," I told her.

We talked some more and the brandy quickly vanished. She refused a second.

"Remember? I have to go home in time to read a script."

"March always keeps his promises," I said. I motioned to

the waiter and he brought the check. We got up and headed for the main entrance. The maître d' hurried across the room to intercept us.

"Was everything to your satisfaction, Miss Mills, Mr. March?"

"As always, Emile," she said.

"Excellent," I added. I slipped him a bill.

"Thank you, sir. I'll have the boy bring your car."

I decided to make it sound easier. "Don't bother. I'll take care of the boy and walk back and get the car myself. The food was so good I'm afraid I ate too much. The fresh air will do me good."

"I hope we'll see you again, Mr. March."

"I imagine you will," I said.

We went on out the door. The doorman sprang to attention.

"Would you like your car, sir?"

"I think we'll try a taxi."

There were a few taxis on the street near the restaurant. He waved his arm and one pulled up to us. I tipped the doorman and we got into the cab. I gave the driver instructions and we pulled away. I smiled to myself as I imagined someone trying hastily to get the word to the men sitting in the parking lot.

Using a roundabout route, we reached my car and transferred to it. There was no evidence of pursuit as we headed up into the hills.

"Now," she said, "what was the meaning of all that?"

"Of all what?"

"Parking your car and taking a taxi."

"Somebody has been following me recently, and I don't

like anyone looking over my shoulder when I'm out with a beautiful woman."

"Are you serious?"

"On both counts."

"But if they were following you, couldn't they just follow the taxi after you parked?"

"They weren't following me just then, because they had lost me. But I was pretty sure that they would know that I was going to be at the Suckling Pig and would expect to pick me up as I left. So we made it a little tougher for them."

She thought about it for a minute. "You mean that you think someone at the restaurant would let them know you were coming or were there?"

"That's the general idea."

She was quiet until we reached her house. "I must get to work on that script," she said, "but you can come in for just one drink if you'd like."

"I like," I said. I followed her into the house.

"Come into the kitchen and I'll make the drinks," she said.

We went in. There was a note propped up on the counter. She read it and laughed. "It's from Doreen. She says, 'Miss Mills: I put a bottle of champagne in to cool. I thought you might like it when you came home. Doreen.' You made quite a hit with her, Milo."

"That's good. I always like to have a friend in the other camp."

She got out two glasses and the bottle of champagne. I opened it and we perched on stools at the breakfast counter and drank. The bottle was empty before we knew it. We slid off the stools.

"Well," I began, and then stopped as I looked at her.

I put out my arms and she came into them. It was a long, slow kiss. I don't know how much the champagne had to do with it, but a fire was building up. Finally she slipped out of my arms and stood looking at me. Her eyes were bright and warm.

"Oh dear," she said, "this isn't the way it was written."

"I didn't know it was written," I said gently. "I thought it was all ad lib."

"And I hardly know you."

"We'll get acquainted."

"What'll I do about my script?" she wailed.

"Don't worry, honey," I said. "I'll read all the male parts."

With our arms around each other we went off toward another part of the house.

SEVEN

Despite the hour I had gotten home the night before, I was up early in the morning. I had a small drink to blow the sleep out of my brain, then put on a pot of coffee and made some eggs and toast. Later, I had my coffee in the living room, even though the decor kept reminding me of Lita Harper. After that, I showered, shaved, and got dressed. I strapped on my gun, shrugged into my coat, and went outside.

I went over the Cadillac carefully. My guess was right. They had installed a new beep box, this time under the hood. I'd thought that they might have found the one I'd thrown out the evening before and, thinking it had fallen off, would try again.

I removed the box, which was fastened to the hood with a magnet, and looked around. Parked next to me was a bright red Porsche. There was no one in sight, and the draperies on all the front apartments were still drawn. I walked over to the Porsche and quickly fixed the box beneath it. That would give them something to follow.

Back in the building I went to the manager's apartment and rang the bell. A pleasant-faced man opened the door.

"I'm Milo March," I told him. "I'm a friend of Jed Moore's and he's letting me use his apartment while he's gone."

He nodded. "Yes, I know, Mr. March. Mr. Moore told me you'd be here. What can I do for you?"

"I am also an insurance investigator. Although I'm supposed to be on vacation, my company has some interest in the incident of the other night and has asked me to look into it."

He looked stricken. "I'm afraid I can't help you much, Mr. March. He moved in about eight months ago. His references were quite good, and I rented him the apartment without knowing who he was. I'm afraid that the owner is very distressed about the whole affair."

"Well, I didn't want to grill you," I told him. "I'm working closely with the police, and they said it would be all right if I looked through the apartment. You may check with Lieutenant Cooper if you like."

"I guess it'll be all right," he said. "Mr. Moore is one of our best tenants and he spoke very highly of you. The sooner this whole thing is over, the better it'll be for us. I'll let you in."

I followed him upstairs and he unlocked the door of the Renaldi apartment. "Just lock the door when you're finished, will you, Mr. March?"

I assured him I would, and he hurried back downstairs. I guess he didn't want to look into the place again. When I went in, I didn't blame him too much. There was a huge stain of dried blood on the wall-to-wall carpeting, and the rest of the apartment was in disarray. The police had probably tried to put everything back in order, but no one could ever accuse them of being tidy housekeepers.

I started in the bedroom. I didn't really expect to find something, but I didn't want to be guilty of overlooking anything. I even felt through all of his jacket pockets in the hope there might be something like a key, but drew a blank. Moving on to the kitchen, I covered every inch of it, then did the same thing with the bathroom and the living room. It was a wasted effort. Locking the door, I returned to the apartment below. I phoned Lieutenant Cooper.

"Milo March," I said when he answered.

"Hello, March," he said. "How's the gumshoe business?"

"About like yesterday. I just finished going through Renaldi's apartment here. Looks as if your boys didn't miss anything."

"They seldom do on something like that. But we're still missing something. It would help if we could find the jewelry. We've been checking through the city to see if Renaldi had any safe-deposit boxes. It's hard work, and so far we haven't found any."

"It would take a lot of boxes to hold that much jewelry."

"It sure would. He'd have to spread the rentals. What's on your mind, March? You must want something or you wouldn't have called."

"As a matter of fact, I do. I'd like to have the addresses of Danny Polerri, George Lotti, and Mack Larry, and some other information about them."

"I can give you their addresses. Just a minute." When he came back on the phone he read off the addresses and I scribbled them down. Two of them were on the same street and the other must have been no more than a block away. All were in the Hollywood area.

"Thanks," I said. "Now I'd like to know what cars they have and the license numbers."

"I don't have those. Get them from Hollywood Vice. Ask for

Lieutenant Whitmore. I'll call and tell him you'll be getting in touch. Is that all?"

"For the moment."

"I'll be waiting impatiently," he said. He hung up before I could thank him.

I poured some V.O. over ice and sipped it while I waited long enough for him to reach the Hollywood police. Then I called and asked for Whitmore.

"My name is Milo March," I said. "Did Lieutenant Cooper call you about me?"

"He did. He said that you were taking over the running of our forces. I guess you forgot to tell Mayor Yorty about it, but we're public-minded. He also told me what you wanted, and I've got it right in front of me. Ready?"

"Go ahead."

The black Ford was Danny Polerri's car. The big gray car that had followed me up Laurel Canyon belonged to Mack Larry. Whitmore gave me the license numbers.

"Now," he said, "George Lotti had a Dodge Dart, but it was cracked up yesterday. Lotti claims it was stolen. One of my men just came in a few minutes ago and said he saw Lotti driving a Ford on Hollywood Boulevard. He wrote down the license number. We like to keep track of things, so we checked it out. The car was listed with a rental service. We called them and they confirmed that Lotti had rented the car late yesterday afternoon." He added the license number, which I wrote down.

"Thanks, Lieutenant," I said.

"Not at all. We like to cooperate with citizens. But remember one thing, March, we don't like to have any laws broken or even bent. Unfortunately, there isn't any open season on men like Polerri, so go easy with whatever you have in mind. That piece of paper you're carrying may not be worth as much as you think it is."

"I'm always careful, Lieutenant," I said. "Good-bye." Next I called the local Intercontinental office and got hold of the young man I'd talked to once. He remembered me. I gave him a rough idea of what I wanted, and he transferred the call to their vice-president, a man named Redland.

"This is Milo March," I told him. "I sometimes work for the home office."

"I've heard of you," he said. "I also know you're working on our jewelry case out here. What can I do for you?"

"Palm National Bank. Do you carry any of their insurance?"

"Most of it. The building, furniture and machines, employees. Why?"

"Do you make regular inspection visits?"

"Of course. It's usually only a formality, but we make them."

"When did you make the last one?"

"Several months ago. I think we're due to make another in about a month."

"I want to visit the bank and ask a few questions without anyone knowing that I'm there because of the jewelry. Do you think we could arrange for me to go on a usual inspection trip?"

"I don't see why not. I can explain that it's early because the home office is sending men around to all the branch offices just to be sure we're doing our job properly. That should do it. I'll call at once and say you'll be there this morning. Ask for Mr. Bayer when you go."

"Thanks. I suppose you have files on the employees?"

"Yes."

"Okay." I hung up and went back to my drink. When I thought enough time had passed, I went out to my car. The red Porsche was gone and I had a happy picture of Danny Polerri following it all over Los Angeles.

The bank was on Wilshire Boulevard. I parked in its lot and went inside. Mr. Bayer proved to be a pleasant young man who was a junior vice-president.

"Glad to meet you, Mr. March," he said. "Your office called and told me you were coming over. We weren't quite expecting you yet, but I don't suppose that'll cause any problem." He chuckled to show that they had no reason to worry about any inspection.

"I'll try not to disrupt anything," I said, "and get out as soon as I can."

"Take all the time you want. What would you like to see?"

"All the usual things," I said vaguely. "And I would like to talk to a few people at random, since this is my first trip here. Why don't I start with you?"

"Fine," he said heartily. "Come in and sit down at my desk."

So I talked with him. In a way I was glad I started there, for it turned out he was one of the people who had to do with safe-deposit boxes. He was in charge of that department, although there were four girls who actually did the work and made the entries in the records.

Then I had to go with him and pretend to be interested in all of their business machines, burglar alarms, and things like that. He also showed me various records while I nodded and made imaginary notes on a piece of paper. We finally ended up back at his desk.

"Fine," I said. "Now, if it's all right, I'd like to wander around and talk briefly to some of the girls. I won't bother anyone who's busy at the tellers' windows."

"Go right ahead," he said. "Only don't try to steal any of the girls. I'm not sure our insurance covers that." He gave another one of his chuckles.

"I'll try to restrain myself," I promised.

I went through the gate again, stopping to talk to a girl who was operating a machine. I didn't pay much attention to what she was saying, but used the talk as a cover while I studied the other girls busily working. I thanked the girl at the machine and started to move on, when something stopped me.

An old woman had just come out of the vault where the safe-deposit boxes were kept and was going out through the bank lobby. She was followed from the vault by a girl I hadn't seen before—although to simply describe her as a girl was not to use the language properly. She was a beautiful blonde. That was also an inadequate description.

The sight of her reminded me of the youth I had met on Carlton Way the evening before. He had mentioned a blonde that Johnny Renaldi had often brought there. He had described her as being strictly from Stacksville. I decided it fitted this girl, too.

I stopped and talked to three other girls and finally made

my way to the blonde, who was sitting at a table working on some records. She looked up as I stopped beside her.

"Hello," I said. "My name is Milo March. I'm making the regular inspection of equipment for the insurance company. It just occurred to me that you're the most valuable-looking bit of equipment in the place."

She smiled. "Thank you. I'm sorry to disappoint you, but I don't think the bank has insured me."

"An oversight. I must take it up with the home office when I get back to New York. What's your name?"

"Hilda Perkins."

"What do you do for the bank?"

"I work in records, and part of the time I work in the safe-deposit department."

"Well," I said, "I'm afraid that doesn't involve anything we insure. I was hoping it was something very involved so that we'd have to discuss it over lunch or dinner."

She laughed, and it was obvious she didn't exactly object to flattery. "Did you say you were from New York?"

"That's right."

"Then why are you here?"

"Every once in a while they send someone like me out to the branch offices to make sure they are not cheating our policyholders. In this case, I'm the one. Up until now I was missing New York and sorry that I came. Now it's all worth it."

This time she not only smiled but gave me a flutter of her eyelashes. I wondered why. I didn't think I was quite that charming and I was certain she didn't have trouble getting men. On the contrary, she probably had to fight them off.

"I've always wanted to see New York," she said. "Do you think I could get a job there?"

"Honey," I said fervently, "you could get a job in the middle of the Gobi Desert. All you'd have to do is stand there until the first camel rider came along."

"I don't know anything about camels," she said seriously, "but I'm pretty good at records. Do you think there might be a job with your company?"

So that was it. "If they refused to give you a job," I told her, "I would be forced to hand in my resignation."

"You're sweet," she said.

I almost winced, but remembered my loyalty to Intercontinental. "I'll be in touch with you," I told her, "sooner than you think. Then we can talk about it. Someone here might get the wrong idea if we talk too long. Okay?"

"Okay," she whispered, fluttering her eyelashes again. I made my way back to the front, stopping to talk to a couple of more girls, but my heart wasn't in it. I finally reached Mr. Bayer.

"Well," he said jovially, "I see you discovered our most outstanding employee."

"Outstanding was just the word I had in mind," I said gravely. "But we were really talking about her work. I want to thank you, Mr. Bayer. You have been most helpful and I'm sure that everyone will be pleased."

"We are always glad to help," he said. "Stop in and see us anytime."

"It may be difficult. I have to go back to New York soon." We shook hands and I left. I stopped outside long enough to get my breath back. Then I found the nearest phone booth and called Mr. Redland at Intercontinental. He came on the phone at once.

"Yes, Mr. March. How did it go?"

"All right, as far as getting through it. I'd like to know something more about one employee."

"I anticipated that you'd have some questions. I have the files of the bank employees in front of me. Which one are you interested in?"

"Miss Hilda Perkins."

"Just a minute." There was a moment of silence, except for him muttering to himself. "I have it. It's a fairly complete report, but I'm afraid that it won't help you much. The investigator states that Miss Perkins is rather startling when viewed as a physical specimen. He implies that her intellectual attainments are not on the same level. Her job history is not above average—unless you count the fact that she entered a beauty contest when she was sixteen. She was a cashier in a restaurant, sold tickets in a motion-picture theater, and then demonstrated cosmetics in a department store. It was while on the latter job that she went to night school and took a business course. She then applied for the job at the bank and was hired about one year ago. Her work is reported as satisfactory."

"Stirring," I said. "As a matter of curiosity, did she win the beauty contest?"

"Yes. She was Miss Avocado for one year."

"Perfect," I said. "What about her personal life?"

"Seems above reproach. Probably for natural reasons, she

has a lot of boyfriends, but there's no evidence of any rumor or scandal. She's never been married. Her parents have been dead for about four years. She lives alone in an apartment with a rent well within her means, where she has been since her parents died. She pays her rent promptly. She occasionally has a date for dinner, but is always home early. She has never thrown a wild party, and no one in the building ever saw a man enter her apartment. All of the neighbors interviewed reported—apparently with reluctance—that her morals were beyond criticism."

"It must have been a strain on her," I muttered.

"Possibly. I might add one thing." He suddenly showed a sense of humor unusual in a vice-president. "I recall that the investigator who worked on this case was breathing heavily for three or four weeks."

I laughed. "Did he recover?"

"I'm not sure. He quit suddenly, saying that his doctor had told him he had to find a less exciting job."

"I can understand it. I've seen the girl. Is that all, Mr. Redland?"

"I'm afraid so. Not much help, is it?"

"Not much. Well, I struggle along. Thanks."

"Good luck," he said.

I got into the car and thought for a minute. I had one specific thing I wanted to do and first things came first, so I headed for an electronics store I knew about. I parked and went inside. I introduced myself and showed my California private detective license.

"What can I do for you, Mr. March?" the clerk asked.

"Well, I'd like to get three beep boxes and a receiver."

His eyebrows went up. "Three beep boxes and one receiver?"

"Yes. Unless it's impossible. I want to be able to get all three boxes on one receiver, and I'd like them to be set at different frequencies so that I can tell which one is which."

"It can be done, but you can't get all three of them at the same time. There would have to be three settings on the receiver, and you would have to switch from one to another."

"That's fine."

"It'll take a few minutes to fix the frequencies and the settings."

"Okay."

"I'll be right back," he said. He disappeared into the rear of the shop. He was back within a couple of minutes. "It won't take Hector long. Anything else, Mr. March?"

"Yes. I want a tape recorder that can be activated by sound and will pick up from a transistor mike at some distance. The tape recorder must be one that can be placed in my car where it will not be easily seen or found."

He pursed his lips. "How much recording time?"

"Probably an hour will be fine, but if we can stretch it a little, so much the better."

"How far away will the mike be?"

"I don't know exactly. Let us say that the recorder will be in the car parked on a street. The mike will be somewhere in a nearby building. A hundred yards should cover all possibilities. I'll want to get the mike too."

"What kind?"

"One that I can either carry in my pocket or can drop somewhere in a room. The latter is probably the best, I suppose."

"How long will the mike have to operate?"

"No more than two hours, I'd guess."

"That's easy. Where would you like the tape recorder in your car?"

"Well, I don't want it easily spotted. On the other hand, I'm driving a rented car, so I don't want an installation that will mar any part of the inside."

He nodded. "How about in the trunk? Perhaps covered by something that seems to be just thrown inside?"

"I think that might be all right."

"Where is your car?"

"It's in your parking lot out back. A white Cadillac. Here's the key to the trunk."

"I'll have Louie install it at once. Do you want the receiver for the beep boxes installed too?"

"No, I'll just carry that on the seat next to me."

He nodded and vanished again. This time he was gone a little longer. When he returned, he gave me back the key.

"It'll be ready in just a few minutes, Mr. March. Now, here's the mike." He handed me an object no larger than a matchbook. "This small button will turn it on. And the first voice after that will activate the tape recorder. You can drop it almost anyplace you wish: alongside the cushion in a chair or couch, placed behind a book, or in any small place of concealment. I gave you a recorder that will pick up clearly from anywhere within one hundred and fifty yards. Anything else, Mr. March?"

I took the microphone and slipped it into my pocket. "Yes, I'd like another tape recorder in a briefcase with a built-in mike. It doesn't have to be an expensive one. I don't expect even to try to use it."

"Ah, I understand, a decoy. I have an excellent one for that purpose. Frankly, it is not too good on performance and is bought only by amateurs. But it should serve well enough for what you have in mind." He went over to a shelf and came back with a nice-looking briefcase. He put it on the counter. I had to admit that it looked great.

"It is ready to operate," he said, "so unless an expert looks at it, no one will know that it's not one of the best. If you want to start it, press down on the lock. That way it will be recording when it's opened. Anything else?"

"I think not."

"May I ask you a question, Mr. March?"

"Sure."

"On the other equipment, do you expect to be near the mike while it is functioning?"

"Yes."

"And you are not certain where your car will be?"

"That's right."

"And I presume that the recordings are important?"

"Yes."

"Ah—may I make a suggestion?" He dived below the counter and came up with something he put on top of it. "What would you say this was, Mr. March?"

I looked at it. "A transistor radio?"

"Quite true. Turn the knob in the correct way and you will

get this." He turned the knob and a second later there was music on it. He shut it off. "But if you turn it the other way, it becomes a tape recorder with its own built-in microphone. It will record for about forty-five minutes. It is one of our newest devices. I suggest one of these. Then, if your car should be too far away or if you put the mike in a bad spot, you will have something else to fall back on."

"All right," I said, "I'll take it."

He gave a birdlike nod and started making out a sales slip. When he had finished, he shoved it across to me. It came to a fair amount. I counted out the money and gave it to him.

He checked it and then looked at me. "I presume you want a duplicate slip?"

"Please."

He nodded again and handed me a yellow slip. He indicated the object on the counter. "You want this wrapped?"

"No. I might as well get used to carrying it." I picked it up and slipped it into my pocket. "Oh, one thing I forgot. Attachments to fasten the beep boxes in place."

"They are included, if you're thinking of magnetic attachments. But I do think you might have overlooked something else."

"What?"

"Extra tape for your two recorders."

I smiled at him and shook my head. "If I get a chance to use either one of them, I won't need more tape immediately. If I don't, I still won't need more tape."

He nodded and darted over to the door that led to the rear of the store. He faced me. "I believe you are ready to go, Mr.

March. It's been a pleasure to serve you. I believe this is the first time you've visited us."

"I'm from New York," I told him. "Maybe I'll see you on my next trip this way."

I left the store and went back to the parking lot. First, I checked the trunk of the car. I almost missed seeing it. There was a piece of burlap tossed far back in the trunk and that was all. I reached out and lifted it. There was the tape recorder, but it didn't even look like a recorder, more like a toolbox. I felt it and discovered it was held in place by magnets. Satisfied, I tossed the burlap back into place and closed the trunk.

When I got behind the wheel, I found a package on the seat beside me. I opened it and took a look. There were the three beep boxes marked 1, 2, and 3. The receiver had two knobs. One was marked Volume, and the other had three settings also marked 1, 2, and 3. I turned the volume to the lowest point and switched the other knob to the first setting. The *beep, beep* came in loud and clear. The same was true of the other two settings. I turned it off, tossed my new briefcase into the back seat, and started the car.

I checked the time as I drove off. It was early enough in the day so that most hoods were probably still asleep. I drove straight to the street where two of them lived and checked the two addresses. Danny Polerri's car was there, parked on the street, but Mack Larry's car was nowhere in sight. He was probably out following a red Porsche.

I parked a couple of buildings away from Danny's address and walked up the street. There was no one on the sidewalk. There was one car coming along. I timed my walking so that the car was gone before I reached the black Ford. I was carrying the first beep box. As I reached the car, I bent over and quickly fixed the box beneath the grille in front. I crossed the street, went back down, and crossed again to the Cadillac. I drove to the other address about a block away. The rented car was parked in front of the building.

I repeated my action with the second beep box. It took only a few minutes to install it. I returned to the Cadillac and tested the receiver. It worked perfectly for both boxes, even though one was at least a block west of me.

I had two more errands I wanted to run. I found a gun store and bought a .25 gun and a leg holster for it. Then I went downtown and had the gun registered. There's nothing like being legal.

Since I was already downtown and it was almost noon, I went over to a restaurant that was run by a retired police lieutenant. He was a nice fellow and I was glad to see him again. Also, the food was good. I cut up a few old touches with the owner and a newspaperman I knew while I ate, and then left.

On the way uptown I stopped off at the apartment I had rented. I had already searched it as thoroughly as I could, but I kept thinking I might get an idea there. I sat down, lit a cigarette, and thought about the case.

There wasn't too much to go on, but there were a few things that stood out. Whether she meant to or not, Lita Harper had unquestionably told Johnny Renaldi where wall safes were located in the various homes. Somebody in the Palm National Bank had tipped Renaldi off to the removal of jewelry from safe-deposit boxes. And another somebody—and I would bet it was Emile Thoret—had let him know when victims came to the restaurant.

I felt certain that Mack Larry had probably opened the safes while George Lotti and Danny Polerri stood guard, despite what Lieutenant O'Brien had said about their reason for riding herd on me. There were only two problems. One was how to pin it on them, and the other was the location of the stolen jewelry. That was enough. If I could only find one little crack in either problem, I might be able to bring both of them down. But where was the crack?

It was time to leave. I drove up to the Palm National Bank on Wilshire and left the car in the parking lot. I got out and waited on the sidewalk not far from the front doors. The blinds were pulled, but I knew that inside all the employees were dusting off the money or whatever it is they do after banking hours are over.

Within a half hour an executive began letting the workers out. The fourth one to appear was Hilda Perkins. Every male eye on the street came sharply to attention. I did more than that. I stepped out to meet her.

"Hello," I said.

"I beg your pardon," she said automatically. Then she took a good look at me. "Oh, Mr. March, I didn't realize it was you. I thought it was somebody trying to be fresh."

"It was," I said. "I was in the neighborhood and thought I'd stop by and see if you'd have dinner with me. It would save me from a lonely meal, and we could talk about your hopes of going to New York."

"It's too early for dinner," she said doubtfully.

"I know. I thought I could drop you off at your place and then return to pick you up at whatever time you say. We could have dinner anyplace you'd like and maybe see a show, and then I'll take you home. We can talk while we're having dinner. Of course, if you already have a date, I'll understand."

"No, I don't have a date." She stared at me for a minute and then smiled. "I think that would be just lovely, Mr. March."

I led her to the car and helped her in, then went around and slid under the wheel. I looked at her. "Which way?"

"I just love Cadillacs," she said, stroking the seat. "Oh! I live on Rossmore. I'll tell you where to go when we get there."

I pulled out into the stream of traffic and headed east. She chattered as I drove and I let her run on without trying to ask any questions. When we reached Rossmore, she told me to turn right, and we finally ended up in front of a medium-sized apartment house.

"I'll be ready in a couple of hours," she said. "It's apartment seven. Just ring the bell and I'll come down."

"This isn't near where you work," I said. "How do you usually go back and forth, by taxi?"

"Oh, no. We don't make enough money for that in the bank. I take the bus every day."

"That must brighten up the morning for a lot of bus drivers."

"Oh, Mr. March! You'll be back in two hours?"

"I'll be here, Miss Perkins."

"You're nice," she said. She opened the door and was gone into the building.

I made a U-turn and headed north on Rossmore. I stayed

on the street when it became Vine. As I drew near Hollywood Boulevard, I reached under the seat and put the receiver beside me. I drove along, turning the receiver on and switching it from one frequency to another. Just before I reached the boulevard, I got a beep from it. I glanced down. Mack Larry's car was parked somewhere near. The beep faded as I drove toward Western and faded out before I got to Bronson. I left it on the rest of the way, but picked up no more sounds.

I had a couple of slow drinks in my favorite bar, talked to some of the regular inmates, and then it was time to go back. I parked in front of Hilda's building, entered the foyer, and rang the bell. Then I waited, feeling a little like a schoolboy on his first date. Maybe I should have just stayed in the car and sounded the horn.

She came out of the elevator within two minutes. I didn't notice what she was wearing, but she looked great, especially in the upper regions.

"My, but you're prompt," she said.

"So are you," I answered. I didn't say any more until we were in the car and headed the other way. "Where would you like to have dinner?" I asked.

"Anyplace you suggest, Mr. March."

"Look, honey," I said, "it's your town, so you tell me where you would like to go. And call me Milo, not Mr. March. It makes me feel like looking over my shoulder to see if my father is standing there."

She laughed. "You're cute. Well, I've heard of a place out in the Valley that's supposed to be very good, but I've never been there. I think it's expensive."

"That's all right, honey. I made a couple of extra dollars today shining shoes. Where is this place?"

"Just the other side of Studio City on Ventura Boulevard. It's called the Gourmet Lodge."

I'd heard of it. She was right. It was expensive. She had probably learned the difference between expensive and ordinary items at a very early age. No matter what the files reported, she was an expensive item.

"Okay," I said. "I hope you don't mind, but I want to stop by my place for a minute. It's not far away."

She glanced at me and the eyelashes fluttered. "You're not really going to pull that corny line, are you?"

"What corny line?"

"Wanting to show me your etchings."

"Haven't an etch in the place," I assured her. "You might think that I'm impolite, but I wasn't going to invite you in. I just want to pick up something. As a matter of fact, I hate hotels, so I rented a furnished apartment for the short time I'm going to be here. I hate housework, so it's a mess."

That put her in a good mood again, and she started chatting about why she wanted to go to New York. I grunted occasionally, but that was all that was necessary, for she was carrying the ball. I drove down Sunset and turned left on Wilton. A block farther on I turned left on Carlton, and I could feel her body stiffen. The flow of words broke off. At the end of the street I made a U-turn and stopped in front of the bungalow apartments.

"Why are you stopping here?" she asked. Her voice was suddenly tense.

"I live here," I said lightly. "It's my little home away from home. I'll only be a moment. You can come and look—from the doorway—if you'd like."

"What apartment?"

"Eight."

"Please—don't be long."

"I won't."

I got out and went to the apartment. I knew she could see which one I entered. I went inside and looked around for a couple of minutes, then returned to the car. She was just sitting there, staring straight ahead. I went back down and took the Harold Way entrance to the freeway. We were at the restaurant within fifteen minutes.

I had a martini and she had a grasshopper. I noticed that her face was almost the same color as the drink. I had a second drink, but she refused another. I was doing most of the talking, word-painting the glory of New York City, although she seemed to have lost her earlier enthusiasm.

The food was fine. I had a steak and she ordered a lobster, but I noticed that she ate only a very small part of it. She also refused dessert and a drink with her coffee. She looked as if she had something on her mind.

"Well," I said when dinner was over, "where would you like to go now? To a nightclub?"

"I—I have a terrible headache," she said. "Would you mind just taking me home? I know I've ruined your evening, but I can't help it. I'm sorry."

"It's all right, honey," I said.

I helped her into her coat and out to the car. I played the

sympathetic man to the hilt on the way back to her place, but her responses were not really with it. She tried to rally when I pulled up in front of her building.

"I'm sorry, Milo," she said again. "I—I'll see you soon." Then she was out of the car and almost running as she went inside.

One thing was certain, I thought as I turned around. Hilda Perkins was the blonde from Stacksville who had visited Johnny Renaldi in his second apartment.

EIGHT

The evening was still young, so I decided to try out something else I had in mind. I drove over to where Danny Polerri and Mack Larry lived. I turned on the receiver but there was no beep, so Polerri wasn't around. I drove up the street, but Larry's car wasn't in sight either. I drove back, parked the Cadillac on Hollywood Boulevard, and walked up the street.

Danny Polerri lived in apartment twenty on the second floor. I checked and discovered it was a corner apartment in the front. I went outside and looked at the windows. There was no light showing. Then I returned to the building. The hallway was deserted. I quickly picked the lock of the apartment and slipped inside. I closed the door quietly and stood for a minute listening while my eyes adjusted to the darkness. There was enough light coming in from the street so that I could finally see pretty well.

I found the bedroom first and made sure that no one was sleeping there. Then I searched it. I didn't find anything interesting—unless you want to call a gun, a sap, and some pornographic pictures interesting. Then I went through the living room, the kitchen, and the closets. Nothing. The nearest thing to jewelry that I found was a tie clasp with a fake ruby in it. I gave up.

Mack Larry's apartment was next. It, too, was in the front

and was empty. And I do mean empty. The only unusual thing in it was a very fine set of tools that would have made any safecracker happy.

I drove to the next block. The receiver indicated that George Lotti's car wasn't around, but I doublechecked it before I went up to his apartment. It was also in the front of the building. Those boys wanted to know who was coming. Lotti had three extra guns in the place and some feminine clothing, but that was all. I couldn't figure out whether he wore the clothes or had a girlfriend who occasionally stayed over.

I drove up to Western Avenue and stopped in at the bar. I had a bourbon and soda, then ordered a second one, and went to the phone and called Kitty Mills.

"I'm auditioning for male parts," I said when she answered.

"You bastard," she said. "I just reached page ten."

"No part for me?"

"You're impossible, Milo," she said. "Where are you? Out with some ravishing blonde?"

"I was out with a ravishing blonde but she suddenly got a headache. Maybe I have problems and nobody will tell me."

"So that's why you're calling me! You couldn't make out."

"That's the story of my life. You know March—in like a lamb and out like a lion."

She laughed. "You couldn't prove it by me. How are you doing on the job?"

"You're the only jewel I've found," I said gravely. "Which reminds me—how would you like to come out for a drink, or an ice cream? I've discovered a place that serves thirty-four flavors."

"No," she said firmly. "I'm going to finish this script tonight. I have to let them know tomorrow. I would love to see you, but it will have to be another night. Will you give me a raincheck?"

"Anytime, honey. I'll call you. Happy script reading." I hung up and went back to my drink. I decided it was just as well. I would go home and think about the case.

Back in the apartment, I undressed and made myself a drink. I turned on the television set and relaxed. The most important step was to try to locate the missing jewelry. If none of it had shown up in the market, then it must be stashed somewhere. I was certain that Johnny Renaldi was the key—but where had he put it? I didn't think too much of Lieutenant Cooper's idea about safe-deposit boxes. Renaldi didn't seem like the type who would hide his loot in a bank. Even though I had checked the apartments of his associates, I doubted he'd trust them.

It also occurred to me that the stuff might be in Hilda Perkins's apartment, but I doubted that he would trust her. I didn't think that Johnny Renaldi had been the sort of man who would trust anyone. On the other hand, someone had trusted him—and may have decided it was a mistake, which would account for the murder.

There had to have been a mastermind behind the robberies, and Renaldi just didn't fit the role. I didn't care much for the police theory either. I could see Lita Harper being suckered into supplying information, but I couldn't believe that she was capable of planning such an operation, and murder was out of the question.

The more I thought about it, the more I was sure that the solution rested with the dead man. And maybe that was why they were so anxious to follow me, so that they'd be around if I turned up the jewelry. That put it squarely in my lap. I had to find the jewelry if I wanted to catch the gang. But how? It was a good question.

I put it out of my mind then. I had a couple more drinks and watched television, then went to bed.

I was up and out early the next morning. I checked the Cadillac and there was no beep box. As I pulled out, I turned on the receiver. But since I still had one beep box unattached, I also watched the rearview mirror. I needn't have bothered. I quickly picked up the beep that showed someone was following me. According to the setting on the receiver, it was George Lotti. Since there wasn't a beep box on my car, he had to be following close enough to see me, but I didn't try to spot him.

I drove steadily down Sunset, watching the traffic lights. Finally I got what I was looking for. The light changed to yellow just before I hit it. I stepped on the accelerator and made it across the intersection. I think someone called me a name, but the following car would have had to stop for the red light. I made a right turn at the next intersection. There was a medical building halfway down the block, with a parking area in the rear. I turned in and parked and listened to the receiver. The beeps got louder and louder, and then began to fade as he drove past the building. I waited until the sound was barely audible, then drove out and headed for Hollywood Boulevard. I didn't pick up any more beeps until I reached the street where Danny Polerri's car was parked.

Mack Larry's car was not too far away. I stopped some distance back of him and walked up the street with my third beep box. There was no one around, and I quickly fixed it beneath the body. I went back to the Cadillac and tested the reception. It worked fine.

I had nothing to go on but the rather vague idea with which I had gone to sleep the night before. I drove up to Carlton Way and went into Renaldi's spare apartment. Even though I had searched it once, I went over it inch by inch again. This time I pounded the paneled walls, thinking there might be a hollow section back of one of the panels. There wasn't. I gave up and flopped down on the couch and lit a cigarette.

The question was a little like the old gag about looking for a lost dog. Where would I go if I were a dog? I tried to figure out what Renaldi might have done when he wanted to hide the jewelry. There had to be a lot of it, so he couldn't just dump it in a dresser drawer.

I was lying there, staring up at the stained and buckling wallpaper on the ceiling, trying to think where I would be if I were a diamond ring. I felt like a method actor.

Something on the ceiling kept bothering me. I finally realized the light was reflecting from one spot where the ceiling and wall joined. I concentrated on it and realized that someone had used Scotch tape to fasten the wallpaper where it had come loose. I don't know why, but it annoyed me. I climbed on the back of the couch and pulled at it. The end of the wallpaper came away in my hand. Suddenly it felt as if somebody were pelting me with pebbles. I lifted my hands to protect my face, lost my balance, and had to jump off the couch. My feet hit something that rolled, and I was flat on the floor.

Sitting there, I looked at the diamonds that literally covered the floor. When I had fully recovered, I started picking them up. Finally I had them all piled up and started counting them. There were more than three hundred. Most of them were small, but they looked as if they were flawless. I got out my list and checked the loose diamonds that had been stolen from Carl Carleton. I couldn't tell if they were the same diamonds or not, but the number was right.

I went around testing the wallpaper wherever it was loose. There weren't any more little goodies, but I had a start. I didn't want to spend the rest of the day walking around with $200,000 in diamonds. I scooped them up and put them in my coat pockets. They made my coat bulge a little, but I didn't have to walk far. I went out to the car and headed for Beverly Hills. I kept the receiver turned on, but there weren't any beeps.

I reached the apartment house with no trouble, went inside, and looked around. There was a Chinese vase filled with artificial flowers on the coffee table. I took out the flowers and put all the diamonds in the vase, then replaced the flowers. It might not be the greatest hiding place in the world, but it would do for the moment.

I made a drink and sat down. I had the diamonds, but I also should be able to learn something from where I'd found them. It partly fitted in with what I had guessed about Johnny Renaldi. He didn't trust anyone, so probably none of the gang knew where the jewelry was. It also brought up an interesting thought. Why were the diamonds hidden separately from the rest of the loot? I wondered if Renaldi had planned on taking them for himself, and if that was why he had been killed.

I picked up the phone and called Lieutenant O'Brien. "Milo March," I said when he answered. "You know, there's a little something I keep forgetting to ask you."

"You want to watch that, March. Forgetting something has toppled more cops than bullets. What is it?"

"Was Johnny Renaldi carrying a gun the night he was killed?"

There was a slight pause. "Yes, he was. Why do you want to know that?"

"Just curious. Why do you suppose he was carrying a gun?"

"How the hell do I know? He probably carried a gun most of the time."

"Even when he was home in his own apartment and wasn't expecting anyone but Lita Harper? If you were going to crawl into the sack with a woman, Lieutenant, would you keep your gun or would you hang it with the rest of your clothes?"

"It might depend on who the woman was," he said. "Renaldi may have been carrying the gun because Harper told him she was through with him and made some threats."

"Nonsense. She had threatened to break up with him before and he always talked her out of it. He would think that he could do it again."

"Well, his gun hadn't been fired, and it was still in his shoulder holster. If you're trying to make a self-defense case for her, it won't work."

"I wasn't trying to make anything. Have you been able to trace the gun to Lita Harper?"

"No. The numbers had been filed off it, but we managed to restore them. It was stolen from a police officer in Arizona ten months ago, so it could have been bought by anyone—including Lita Harper."

"And everyone else who wanted a gun for illegal reasons," I reminded him. "But I wasn't asking in order to make a case for Miss Harper. It's true that I don't think she killed Renaldi, but I'm more interested in seeing the case solved than in merely trying to destroy your theories. We're really on the same side of the fence, Lieutenant. My company is interested in Lita Harper to the extent of half a million dollars; we're interested in the missing jewelry to the extent of two million dollars. The solution of one problem is the solution of both."

"Okay. Are you getting at something?"

"I hope so—but I don't know what yet. When I do, I'll let you know."

"You'd better. So far you haven't told me anything I didn't know, unless you want to count your half-baked ideas."

"That's why I won't tell you any more. You think all of my ideas are half-baked. In a way, that's true. So I'll serve them to you when they are fully baked."

"Well, keep the oven burning," he said, laughing at his own wit. Then he hung up.

"Cops," I muttered to myself.

I lit a cigarette and went back to thinking. I had an idea which I thought might be pretty good. First, however, I wanted to do something about taking care of Milo March. I picked up the phone book and found the address of the Excelsior Mutual Insurance Company. Their offices were on Santa Monica Boulevard in Beverly Hills. It was still early, so I got in the car and drove over there.

It took a little time to get through to anyone, but I didn't mind, for the scenery in the person of the secretary was nice. Finally, I was shown into the office of a man who was in charge of claims.

"What can I do for you, Mr. March?" he asked after he had given me a limp handshake.

I put my identification on his desk. "I'm a private detective from New York. I also have a license to practice in California. I specialize in insurance cases. Normally I work most of the time for one company, which is Intercontinental."

"I know," he said. "I know your name and of your work."

"I'm working on a case out here for Intercontinental. I have reason to believe that it is a case in which you are also interested. I thought I might be able to represent your interests at the same time."

"Jewelry?" he asked.

I nodded. "That's the case. Do you have someone working on it?"

"Just our staff investigator. What did you have in mind?"

"I'm already getting a per diem and expenses, so I'm not asking for a retainer. But if I also look after your interests, I would expect some compensation out of it."

"Naturally. At the moment we are liable for slightly more than one million dollars on policies covering jewelry stolen in Beverly Hills by what the police believe to be a ring. I have the authority to offer you one percent on the recovery of any of the jewelry which we have insured."

"Good enough. May I have a list of the jewelry you have insured?"

"Certainly." He picked up his phone and told someone to bring in the list. "Would you like a letter confirming this?"

I looked at him and decided to play it the sporting way. "I don't think that's necessary, Mr. ..."

"Hennessey," he supplied.

"I presume you'll send through a memo to your home office and that will be all that's necessary."

He looked pleased. "Very well, Mr. March."

The door opened and a girl came in with some papers in her hand. She placed them on the desk, glanced at me, and left. I watched her as she walked out. It was a pleasant view.

"All right, Mr. Hennessey," I said, standing up. "When I recover the jewelry, I'll let you know."

"When?" he asked, lifting his eyebrows.

"When," I repeated firmly. "I expect to recover it."

"Good. I like that attitude, Mr. March. I will get a memo off to the New York office over the teletype immediately."

"I'll be in touch with you," I told him.

On the way downtown I switched over to Wilshire. It was almost noon and I decided to stop at the bank and invite Hilda Perkins to lunch—just to see how she had recovered from her shakes the day before. I pulled into the parking lot and entered the bank. I looked around but didn't see her.

"Hello, Mr. March," a voice said. I looked over and it was

the junior executive, Mr. Bayer. "Do you need some more information for your report?"

"No," I said honestly. "As a matter of fact I stopped by to see if Miss Perkins would like to have lunch with me."

He barely managed to suppress a leer. "I'm sorry, but she's not in today."

"Oh?" I said. "Is she ill?"

He frowned. "No. Actually, it's very strange. She phoned in this morning and said that her sister was very ill in Oklahoma. She had to go there to take care of her, she said, and she'd be back in a couple of weeks."

"So what's the problem?"

"I checked our records and there is no mention of a sister on her application. We don't mind giving our employees a leave of absence in such cases, but it does seem rather odd."

"It certainly does," I agreed. "Well, if I'm still in town I'll see her when she gets back. Good-bye, Mr. Bayer." I went out and looked for the nearest public phone booth. There was one a block away. I entered it and phoned Lieutenant Cooper in Beverly Hills.

"What do you want?" he asked when he heard my name.

"Nothing," I said. "I called to give you some information."

"That's a switch. What is it?"

"Who checked the employees at the Palm National Bank?"

"I did, but that sounds like asking for information instead of giving it."

"Remember a girl named Hilda Perkins?"

"Yeah," he grunted. "The sexpot."

"That's the one. If I were you, I'd start looking for her—

although it's possible she's already left town."

His tone changed. "How do you know?"

"I just came from the bank. She phoned them this morning and said she had to go take care of a sick sister in Oklahoma and she wanted a leave of absence."

"So what's wrong with that? A lot of people take care of their relatives."

"She doesn't have a sister. At least, not according to her application for work."

"What's it all about?" he asked sharply.

"I had a date with her last night. She said she wanted to try to get a job in New York and she thought I might help her. On our way to dinner I stopped off at the apartment Johnny Renaldi had in Hollywood. She got very upset. I expected her to. Earlier, a young man who lives in one of the apartments gave a perfect description of her as a girl he saw Renaldi bring there often. I took her to dinner, but she had lost her appetite and her desire to talk about New York. She said she had a headache and wanted to go straight home after dinner. Then she called the bank this morning and said she couldn't come to work."

"Interesting."

"She also worked in the safe-deposit box department at the bank. And she knew Johnny Renaldi."

"You might have something, March. She did seem clear when we checked her."

"I know," I said. "She's a good girl. Or was until she met Johnny Renaldi. Or no one knew she wasn't until now. Take your choice."

"I'll check her out right away. Anything else?"

"Not at the moment. Maybe later."

"Okay. Thanks, March."

I went back to the car and drove downtown, switching over to Hollywood Boulevard. I kept using the receiver, but got no response that would indicate the trio were anywhere near me. Once I was below Western Avenue, it didn't take me long to find the building where Renaldi had lived before moving to Beverly Hills. It was an old building, but still in good condition. I parked and went in, looking for the manager.

She turned out to be a gray-haired, slightly plump lady. She was still struggling to get her hat on as she opened the door. "Oh, I'm sorry," she said, "I was just getting ready to go to the store. I'm afraid that we don't have any vacancies, if that's what you're looking for."

"Not exactly," I told her. "I wanted to ask you a couple of questions about a former tenant, if I may."

"Collection agency?" she asked.

I shook my head and took out my identification from Intercontinental. I let her take a good look at it. "This is a matter of insurance. The tenant was John Renaldi."

"Oh, you mean the man who was killed the other day?" She didn't wait for my nod. "He always seemed very nice, and I never knew he was all those terrible things they said in the newspaper."

"I'm not concerned with those things," I said briskly. "Did he live here long?"

"Slightly more than a year, but he moved about eight months ago. He was always a good tenant. Paid his rent promptly and never was one for making a lot of noise. I should know. He lived right above me, in twelve."

"Would you know anything about his relatives?"

She shook her head. "He never mentioned them. Was it a large policy?"

"Pretty large," I said, which was certainly true. "What about his friends?"

"I never saw any of them, but I'm sure he must have had many friends. He was a very charming man."

"I'm sure of that," I said gravely. "Who took the apartment when he gave it up? One of his friends?"

"Oh no. A very nice gentleman who just happened to come in to ask if we had a vacancy. As a matter of fact, he stopped in to ask the day before Mr. Renaldi moved out. A Mr. L.J. George. He's a perfect tenant."

"You mean he's still here?"

"Oh, yes. Well, not exactly, if you mean at the moment. But he still has the apartment."

"I don't understand."

"Mr. George is a traveling salesman, so he is very seldom here, but he wanted to have a home, someplace where he could keep his possessions and a place to stay when he does come back to the city. That's not very often, the poor man. I don't think I've seen him once since he moved in, although I hear him up there once in a while when he comes in late. And the rent is always here the first of every month. He leaves it in my mailbox."

"Sounds like a perfect tenant," I said. "Can't throw many wild parties if he's never here."

"Oh, he's a perfect gentleman, Mr. George is. I knew he was the minute I saw him."

"How did you know that?" I asked politely.

"Just by the looks of him. Handsome he is. About your size, maybe a little heavier. Well dressed, and he has a very neatly cropped mustache."

Something about that description caught my attention and I suddenly stopped just being polite. "You say you've never seen him since he moved in?"

"Haven't seen him, but I've heard him. He arrives sometimes in the evening and I hear him moving around. But then he's usually gone by the time I get up in the morning. He's a real worker."

"I think he is," I murmured. "And he keeps his things up there?"

"Yes, indeed. He moved in several large suitcases. But he only takes one small bag with him on his trips. He told me so himself."

"That sounds very interesting."

"Oh, my dear," she exclaimed. "Here you came around to ask about poor Mr. Renaldi's family and I keep talking about another tenant. I'm sorry."

"It is I who should apologize to you," I told her. "I've been keeping you from your shopping. Thank you for your help."

"I hope you find what you're looking for, young man," she called after me as I left.

Outside I stopped and looked around. If she was going shopping, she'd probably have to go to Hollywood Boulevard. I turned and walked slowly in the opposite direction. I kept looking back as I walked. I was almost to Franklin when I saw her leave the building and trot off toward the boulevard. I turned and walked swiftly back to the building.

I went directly to the second floor and to apartment twelve. I picked the lock and let myself inside. The place had a musty smell, as though no one had lived there in a long time. A quick look through the rooms tended to bear that out. There was dust everywhere. Even the bed was dusty, and obviously had not been slept in for some time. There were ashtrays in the living room and the bedroom, but they had not been used recently. There were no visible signs that anyone lived there.

Finally, I started looking in the closets. In the third one I found what I was looking for. Four suitcases were stacked on the floor. I dragged one outside and opened it. It was full of jewelry. I didn't have to check through it to know that this was the missing loot. I closed the suitcase and crossed to the window and looked out. The manager was not in sight and would certainly be gone for several more minutes, if not longer.

I carried two of the suitcases downstairs and put them in the Cadillac. I went back and got the other two, locking the door after me and using my handkerchief to remove any prints I had left on the knob. I went downstairs and put the two bags with the first ones. Then I got in and drove away.

I parked the car at the Beverly Hills police station and locked the doors. Then I went inside to see Lieutenant Cooper. He looked up sourly as I entered his office.

Well," he said, "it looks as if you might have had the right idea. The Perkins girl has skipped out, but she was caught at

International Airport. They're bringing her in now. I suppose you want something in return for the tip?"

"On the contrary, Lieutenant. I come bearing gifts. I have something more for you, but I want your promise that nothing will be released to the newspapers during the next twenty-four to forty-eight hours."

"Give it to me. If your request is reasonable, I'll go along with it."

"Get a couple of strong detectives and come out to my car," I told him.

He raised his eyebrows, but stood up. "Come on," he said. "This better be good, March."

"It is."

We walked down the corridor to a large room in which several detectives were waiting for assignments. The Lieutenant called to two of them and they followed us outside, looking at me curiously. I unlocked the car and threw open a rear door. "There's my present."

"What the hell is it?" Cooper asked.

"Why not take it inside and open it—or them? I suggest you use a larger room than your office."

He nodded to the two detectives and they carried the suitcases inside. We followed them into the room from which we had collected the detectives.

"Open them," the Lieutenant ordered.

A moment later we were all standing there looking at four jumbled piles of jewels.

"Holy Jesus," one of the detectives muttered.

"Where'd you get it?" Lieutenant Cooper asked. He didn't

have to ask what it was; he knew.

"Remember where Johnny Renaldi lived before he moved to Beverly Hills?"

"I ought to. I gave you the address."

"Well, that's where it was. Hidden in a closet."

"You mean the apartment has never been rented to another tenant?"

"It has been. I'm not completely certain about the story, but it was rented the day before Renaldi moved out to a man who called himself L.J. George. Mr. George claimed that he was a traveling salesman and would seldom be in the apartment, but that he wanted a permanent home base. The lady who manages the building has never seen her tenant since he moved in, but she says she has heard him there a few times. And, she added, he always leaves the rent in her mailbox the first of every month."

"Who the hell is L.J. George?"

"I'm not sure, Lieutenant, but the description sounds like that of George Lotti. My guess would be that Renaldi sent him around to rent the apartment. Once that was accomplished, Renaldi took over the key and slipped the rent into the mailbox every month. The tenant the manager occasionally heard was Renaldi, who dropped around to add to his store of goodies or maybe just to run barefooted through the collection. If it was Lotti who rented it, the manager can identify him."

"We'll pick him up," the Lieutenant said grimly.

"No newspaper stories, Lieutenant?" I asked.

"Why?"

"There are a few jewel thieves who have to be rounded up.

I have an idea it'll be easier if they don't know their old-age benefits have vanished into the arms of the law."

"All right. We'll hold up the story for at least a day."

"Thanks, Lieutenant. Now, there is one more thing …"

He looked at me with suspicion. "What?"

I waved at the jewelry. "I'd like a receipt for this."

A touch of color began to creep into his face. "A receipt? What the hell does that mean? Do you think we're going to steal the stuff?"

"No, Lieutenant. But I have to report to my people that I have recovered the jewels they insured and have turned them over to you. They, in turn, will have to report to the policy-holders. My report will have to be itemized so that they will know everything is here. You're going to have to check all of this stuff against the lists you have, so it will be simple then to give me a receipt for it."

"It'll take us at least two hours to go over all of it."

"I'll wait."

"I'll be damned if you will. You'll get out of here and come back later. I'll have your receipt for you."

"My people have a lot of money involved here."

He glared at me, then got a grip on himself. "Look, March, you did a good job finding this stuff and I'm grateful, but you're beginning to get in my hair. Go somewhere and have lunch or something, anything but staying here and getting underfoot while we're working on the recovered property."

"I can hardly get in your hair and underfoot at the same time," I pointed out. But I could see that he wasn't in a mood to appreciate my logic, so I got out.

I drove to the Beverly Hilton and went inside. It always upsets me to be yelled at by policemen, so I had a couple of cool dry martinis to settle my nerves. I even had a third one while my lunch was being brought. Later, I lingered over coffee and brandy.

Driving back to the police station, I felt pretty good about the whole thing. It had been a fair day's work, even though there were still a few loose ends floating around.

Lieutenant Cooper and his men were just finishing up when I entered the big room. The suitcases were once more closed and the men looked tired but relieved.

"There you are," Cooper said. "You'll be pleased to know that everything is here except one item."

"What's that?"

"The loose diamonds which were stolen from Mr. and Mrs. Carleton. Not one of them was in the suitcases."

"You mean you let more than three hundred diamonds trickle through your fingers?"

"You heard what I said, March. Not one of them was in the suitcases. I don't know where they are, but they sure as hell aren't here."

"What are you going to do with what is here?"

"Put it in a bank until we can return it."

"And what about my receipt?"

"It'll be here any minute," he said. The door opened and an officer entered carrying several sheets of paper. "Here it is now." Cooper took the sheets over to a desk, initialed each page, and scrawled his name on the last one. He shoved them toward me. "Here you are. Now get to hell out of here and let me do my work."

I smiled at him. "All right, Lieutenant. I'll see you soon."

"That's what I'm afraid of. But give me a few hours in which to recover."

I drove straight back to my apartment. When I was inside I made sure that the door was locked and bolted, then took my clothes off and stretched across the bed for a nap. I felt I had earned it.

I awakened two hours later feeling refreshed. I padded into the kitchen and made myself a drink and carried it into the living room. I pulled the phone toward me and dialed Kitty Mills's number. This time she answered it herself.

"Aren't we getting democratic," I said, "answering the telephone ourselves! Or are you afraid I'll make a date with Doreen if she takes the call?"

"I wouldn't be a bit surprised," she said. "You look like the sort of man who used to go around ruining working girls."

"I've often thought about it. The only reason I never took it up was that there was no future in it. No, I think it makes a better hobby than a career."

She laughed. "The trouble is that I'm not certain you aren't serious. Hello, Milo darling."

"Hello, Kitty darling," I said gravely. "How was the script?"

"Awful—but it's a good part for me, so I'm going to take it. I told my agent today. How's your job?"

"Oh, I march from obstacle to obstacle. But I think I made enough money today to blow you to dinner tonight."

"I thought you'd never ask."

"I'll pick you up about seven."

"Better make it seven-thirty so I'll have time to put my face on."

"On the other hand, think of the sensation I'd cause if I showed up with a faceless girl. Okay, honey. I'll be there at seven-thirty."

I hung up, waited a couple of minutes, and then phoned the Suckling Pig. I asked for Emile. When he answered, I made a reservation for eight o'clock. He sounded happy to hear from me. I bet he was, too.

I shaved and showered and put on fresh clothing. It was still too early to leave. I fixed another drink and sipped it until it was time. I rummaged through a small Chinese-style desk in one corner of the room and found an envelope. Lifting the flowers from the vase, I shook one diamond into my hand and dropped it into the envelope. I wet the flap, sealed it, and put it in my pocket. Then, replacing the flowers, I left.

The maid opened the door for me. She gave me her best smile and told me that Miss Mills would be right down, and asked if she could get me a drink while I waited. I was tempted to say yes just to give her something to do, but I didn't. Kitty was coming down the stairs almost before the maid was out of the room. I looked at her appraisingly.

"I think," I said, "that the new face is even nicer than the last one I saw. Maybe you should keep this one."

She wrinkled up her nose at me. "Flattery will get you nowhere, my good man. Let's go. I'm famished."

"I never knew a woman who wasn't." I held the door for her and we walked out to the car. "The Suckling Pig all right?" I asked her. She gave me a sharp look but merely nodded.

This time I drove straight to the restaurant and turned the car over to the parking attendant. We went inside and were given the same table we'd had before. I forgot about business until we'd gone through our drinks and the dinner. Kitty decided to have dessert, so I excused myself and went to the rear of the building. Again I slipped out the back door and stood in the shadows.

I soon spotted them, two men sitting in Danny Polerri's black Ford. I moved down to the end of the building, staying in the dark where it was possible to duck down behind a line of cars and get around in back of the Ford without being seen. I took my gun from its holster and moved up on the driver's side of the car, taking care not to scuff my feet on the asphalt. I could hear the low murmur of their voices.

"All right," I said, taking the last few steps. "Both of you keep your hands where I can see them and nobody will get hurt. Hello, Danny. Were you looking for me?" There was enough light so that I could see the second man was Mack Larry.

For a full minute the three of us remained silent and motionless, staring at each other. The silence was finally broken by Polerri's cursing.

"Who do you work for, Danny?" I asked.

"Nobody," he snapped. "I work for myself."

"Johnny Renaldi was your boss until he was killed, wasn't he? Did his death earn you a promotion?"

"Go to hell, March."

"I've got a little present for whoever you work for. I think somebody will find it very interesting."

I took the envelope from my pocket and tossed it into Polerri's lap. "Be sure to pass it along with my compliments. Now, don't try to be a hero."

NINE

Backing away from the car, I returned the same way I had come, making certain that I was facing them. I kept my gun out even though I was sure they wouldn't try anything just then. I could hear their voices but not what they were saying. I held the gun in my hand until I'd reached the rear door of the restaurant. Then I dropped it into the holster and entered.

Kitty looked at me as I sat down. "You were gone so long I was about to ask Emile to send out a rescue team."

"Sorry," I said. "I was having a little visit with a couple of friends."

"In the men's room? What kind of friends do you have, Milo?"

"I paid a visit to two men who were sitting in a car in the parking lot with some idea of following us when we left. I think, perhaps, one of them is the man who opened your safe and the other one stood watch outside while he was doing it."

"Why," she asked in surprise, "would you want to talk to them?"

"That's my job, honey."

"Oh?" She thought about it for a minute. "You really mean that, don't you, Milo?"

"I mean it." I motioned to the waiter and ordered coffee and brandy for us. I waited until he was gone. "This isn't a screenplay. It's for real. Your missing jewelry is real. So is the murder charge against Lita Harper. And so is the work that has to be done to solve the crimes."

The waiter brought coffee and brandy and drifted away. "Is that why you're carrying a gun under your jacket?"

"You noticed?"

She giggled. "It's difficult for a girl to be kissed by a man who's carrying a gun and not notice it. Besides, I've been in a lot of pictures where the leading man carried a gun. I guess there were blank bullets in it."

"These aren't blank," I told her. "Just don't get the make-believe world of your movies mixed up with reality. I don't want you to get hurt."

"Really?"

"Really. And the next twenty-four hours are apt to get a little rough."

"That's why you did the business with the taxi the other night?"

"Yes."

"What about tonight? Won't they follow us?"

"I don't think so. I believe I gave them something else to think about, and they are probably already gone. But it'll start again in the morning. I'll try to keep you out of it by staying away from you as long as it lasts."

"I wouldn't like that, Milo. Besides, it sounds exciting."

"But it's not a script, Kitty. You leave it to me. Now, finish your coffee and brandy and I'll take you home."

"Yes, Milo," she said meekly. But the expression in her eyes was not so meek.

We finished, and this time I let Emile pass orders down the chain of command for the parking attendant to bring my car. We paraded out through the restaurant, handing out money to various underlings, and finally arrived at the car. I gave the boy more money, and we drove away. I didn't see anything of the black Ford, but I took the receiver from under the front seat and turned it on. There was no sound from any of the three positions.

"What's that?" Kitty asked.

"An electronic gadget that would let us know if we were being followed."

"And?"

"We're not, so you can relax."

I drove to her house and we went in. As soon as the door closed behind us, she was in my arms. There was more violence in her body than passion, and it exhausted itself quickly. Then we went into the kitchen to sit at the bar and drink the champagne which the maid had again cooled for us. When the bottle was empty, I took her hand and we wandered out of the kitchen.

I was in no big rush to get up early the following morning. I awakened slowly, finally went into my kitchen, and made some breakfast. I followed it with a cup of coffee. Then, leaving the coffeepot plugged in, I got dressed and went out to check my car. There was another beep box fixed to it, this time underneath the rear end. I left it there and returned to the apartment. I poured a second cup of coffee and lit a cigarette. Then I went into the living room and picked up the phone. I put in a collect call to Martin Raymond at Intercontinental in New York. He came on right away.

"Milo, boy," he said, "how are things going?"

"The way things always go. I've got your jewelry."

"I knew I could depend on you." He sounded twenty years younger. "All of it?"

"All of it."

"Where is it?"

"The police have all of it except the loose diamonds, which were covered on one policy. I have a receipt for what the police have."

"What about the diamonds?" he asked anxiously.

"I have those, too. In fact, they're right in front of me in the apartment where I'm staying."

"What? Those diamonds are insured for two hundred thousand dollars. What are you doing with them in your apartment?"

"Letting them trickle through my fingers. And using them as bait. Don't worry. I'll turn them over to the police in good time."

"What do you mean by bait?"

"Well, I still have to round up the thieves and the person who really killed Johnny Renaldi. You did want me to do that, didn't you?"

"Of course," he said hastily. "I was going to ask you about Miss Harper."

"I feel certain that everything will be neatly trussed up for you before the day is over. Now I'd like you to mail a check to me today."

"A check? Today?"

"You're reading me clear and loud. That's a check for the

per diem money due and the bonus you promised me. Mail it, special delivery, to your local office. Then I can pick it up when I show them the receipt for all the jewelry and they've checked with the police."

"But what's the rush, Milo? You can't be that broke already."

"I was on my vacation, remember, when you dumped this in my lap. Well, the minute this is over I'm going back on vacation, only somewhere so lost that you can't find me for another emergency."

"But—"

"Martin," I interrupted gently, "I have the diamonds here with me. I could take my bonus in a few choice stones. Think about it." I replaced the phone.

I had one drink for the road and then finished dressing. This included strapping on my leg holster and slipping the automatic into it. I wore the other holster and gun in their usual position. I made sure that I had the transistor microphone I had bought, then went out to the car.

I turned on the receiver as I pulled away from the building. There was a loud, clear beep, so I knew I was being followed. I turned the receiver off and put it under the front seat. Then I reached into the back seat and got the briefcase, putting it beside me.

The next problem was to make it easy for them. I finally decided to turn up into the hills. As soon as I was well away from the more congested area, I deliberately picked a small street that looked completely deserted. I followed it about a half mile, then pretended to be having engine trouble, and pulled to the side of the road. I got out and lifted the hood. I could see the Ford not far away, but I ignored it as I stuck my head under the hood and waited patiently.

Out of the corner of my eye I saw the nose of the Ford come into sight and stop.

"Having car trouble?" Danny Polerri asked.

I pretended not to recognize the voice. "It's all right now," I called cheerfully. I backed away and put my hands on top of the hood to close it. Only then did I look at Danny and appear to recognize him. Mack Larry was driving the car.

"What are you doing here?" I asked.

"Seeing that you don't get into trouble," he said. He was pointing a gun at me. "Just hold it the way you are. I like it that way." He got out of the car and came around behind me. He felt for my gun and took it from the holster. "Now you can close the hood. Only don't make any sudden moves."

I closed the hood and stood there. "You can't get away with this," I said.

"We are. Now walk around and get under the wheel of your car."

I did as he ordered. He opened the door on the other side and slid in next to me. His gun was pointed at me, held low enough so that it couldn't be seen from outside.

"Just do as you're told," he said, "and maybe you'll live for a while."

"You talk big when you're holding a gun, Danny."

"You'll see how big I talk, buster. Get this crate moving and turn it around."

I drove back down the hill and followed his directions until we ended up on Sunset Boulevard. I turned right and drove on Sunset. I could see the Ford following closely behind. When we reached the end of Sunset, where it runs into the Pacific Highway, he told me to turn right. Shortly after we'd reached Malibu, we came to a rather large house, right on the ocean, which was surrounded by a fence. He told me to turn into the driveway. I made a left turn and ended up in front of the closed gate.

"Blow the horn," he ordered.

I did so and the gate swung open. I drove inside and the Ford followed. The gate closed. We waited until Mack Larry was out of the car.

"Get out," Danny said, prodding me with the gun.

I opened the door and got out, taking the briefcase with me. Danny got out and came around the car. He waved the gun at me. "Let's go inside, buster. Just open the door and walk in."

I opened the door and stepped into a long corridor running through the house. There was a half-open door on one side leading into what seemed to be a kitchen.

"Straight ahead," Danny said from behind me.

I walked along the corridor until we came to a huge, expensively furnished living room. Danny motioned me inside. There was a man there sitting in a chair, but I couldn't see his face.

"Go across and sit on the couch," Danny ordered me.

I walked across the room and put the briefcase on the floor. As I did so, I pushed the lock so that the tape recorder would start working. Turning around to sit down, I got the transistor mike from my pocket and pushed the switch on it. I dropped it down between the cushion and the armrest of the couch, and then for the first time looked at the man who was seated opposite me. I was not especially surprised.

"Hello, Mr. Carleton," I said.

He ignored me and looked at Danny Polerri. "What's he doing with that briefcase?"

"I don't know, boss. He had it in the car with him and just brought it along."

"See what's in it."

Danny came over and picked up the briefcase. He opened it and cursed when he looked inside. "It's a tape recorder and he's got it turned on."

"Give it to me."

Danny handed it over and Carleton shut it off. He placed it on the floor and looked at me. "It was childish to think you could get away with something like that, March. But what interests me is why did you have it with you? Were you expecting to be picked up?"

"It occurred to me that it might happen."

He nodded. "And you didn't seem especially surprised to see me."

"I wasn't exactly. I had decided before that there was someone who was the mastermind of the jewelry thefts and who had no open contact with the other members of the gang. It had to be someone also who had access to enough money to keep the members supplied with the necessities while the stolen jewels were kept off the market. Then I like to think that Johnny Renaldi gave me a clue—although I was not certain of it."

"What do you mean?" he demanded suspiciously.

"I never knew Johnny, but he must have had some sense of humor. When he rented his second apartment he found one on Carlton Way. I doubt that that was an accident."

"Renaldi was a stupid fool. Useful at times, but stupid." He reached in his pocket and pulled out the diamond I had given Danny the night before. "Where did you get this, March?"

"I found it."

"And you gave it to Danny last night. Why?"

"I thought it would make you interested in seeing me." His gaze swung back to Danny. "Are you sure you weren't followed out here?"

"Mack was covering our rear."

"Nobody followed us," Mack said.

"All right." Carleton looked at me again. "Why did you give the diamond to Danny?"

"I wanted to meet you."

"Why?"

"I couldn't solve the case without knowing all the players."

"Is this one diamond all that you found?"

"No," I said cheerfully, "I found them all."

"Where?"

"In Johnny Renaldi's Carlton Way apartment."

"That's impossible. We searched it and so did the police without finding anything."

"But I did."

"Where are the rest of them now?"

I smiled. "I like to think of that as being my little secret."

"Want me to work him over?" Danny asked. "I'll make him talk."

"I doubt it," I said. "If I told you where to find the diamonds, you'd merely kill me as soon as you got them. You'd have to so that I couldn't tell anyone that Carl Carleton is an ordinary jewel thief. If I don't tell you where they are, you'll probably kill me anyway—but at least you won't get the diamonds."

"Ask him if he knows where the rest of the stuff is," Mack said.

"Shut up," Carleton growled.

I laughed. "You don't have to worry, Mr. Carleton. I know that you don't know where any of the jewelry is. In fact, I have a pretty good picture of the whole operation from beginning to end. Would you like to hear it?"

"Go ahead. It might amuse me."

"When you first started this, Johnny Renaldi was the only one who knew about you. You planned the jobs and Johnny was your front man. He lined everyone else up. He got Lita Harper to give him what she knew about the interiors of the houses. He recruited Hilda Perkins to let him know when anyone removed their jewelry from the bank vaults. It's easy to figure out how he lined them up."

"Yeah," Danny Polerri said. "Johnny was big with the broads."

"But he also lined up Emile Thoret at the Suckling Pig, right?"

"Right," Danny said again. "The guy likes to bet the ponies, and the bookie takes him to the cleaners. Johnny got the bookie to go easy on Thoret and then gave him the chance to make a buck or two."

"Polerri, you talk too much," Carleton said. "If March is so smart, let him tell us how it worked. Don't give him any free answers—not that it really makes any difference."

"I had it figured like that anyway," I told him. "It had to be some hold over him, and gambling seemed the best bet. The reason isn't important. It was obvious that someone at the restaurant was in on it, and all that concerned me was who."

"How'd you get on to him?" Danny asked.

"Easy. I made a reservation there the other night and some-one let you know. You were there waiting for me when I was through with dinner. I was given a choice table even though Emile didn't know me. And he was just a little bit too anxious about me getting my car."

"Stupid!" Carleton snarled. "I told you, Polerri, that you were being stupid the way you were handling this."

"Hey, who're you calling stupid?" Danny said. "I don't have to take that kind of talk. I never saw you until Johnny was dead and you got in touch with me. I can get along if I never see you again."

"That proves you're stupid," Carleton said. "You're in it and you can't get out unless we're completely successful. For your own sake you'd better do the best you can to follow orders. Leave the thinking to me."

"And you're a fine mastermind, Mr. Carleton," I said. "Look at your gang. First there is you, Carl Carleton, successful criminal lawyer, who obviously thinks he has learned so much from his clients that he can become a successful crim-inal. And who obviously needs money badly enough to try it. Johnny Renaldi, a second-rate hood whose specialty had probably always been blackmail and double-crossing and who practiced one of his specialties once too often. Danny Polerri, another small-time hood, whose chief claim to fame is that he once ran errands for a big shot in the Syndicate. Mack Larry, a first-rate safecracker who is trying to survive in a dying profession. Lita Harper, who was trapped by having a case of hot pants. Hilda Perkins, who had hot pants and a desire to go somewhere—and who has been picked up by the cops while trying to pull a sneak. Emile Thoret, who has a passion for slow horses. And, of course, George Lotti—incidentally, where is our George?"

"He was picked up by the cops for questioning," Danny said automatically.

"A nice crew," I said.

Carleton's face had slowly turned red while I had been talking. "Are you quite through, March?" he asked acidly.

"No, but you may speak."

His face got even redder. "You are even more stupid, March. You dare to talk like that when you are our prisoner here? We also have your silly tape recorder and your gun. No one followed you here. You should be begging for your life at this moment."

"Do you mind if I smoke?" I asked.

"Go ahead and smoke!" He almost shouted it.

I took out a cigarette and lit it. "I was talking only because you said you might find it amusing to hear my idea about what had happened."

He rolled the diamond between his fingers, then gestured impatiently. "Go ahead. I have more time than you do."

"I can only guess at one part of it," I said. "I'm sure that you had a good reason for not trying to sell the jewelry immediately. It must have been pretty good, for you to lay out money for your gang to live on—especially since I suspect that you are already mortgaged to the hilt. But you must have had a plan to get more than you could get from the regular fences. And you must have thought it safer. My guess would be that you had Europe in mind. You were probably smart as long as you stuck to plans on paper, but when you moved beyond that, you made a couple of mistakes."

"What?" he snapped.

"The first one was that you were afraid to have the jewelry around you in the event that something went wrong. So you gave Johnny Renaldi the responsibility of hiding the jewelry and neglected to find out where he had hidden it. I can only guess at the second mistake. But I think that you decided to keep the loose diamonds, which were stolen from your house, for yourself. They would be easy to dispose of and you would collect for them twice, as well as taking a major cut of the rest of the jewelry. But you were going to let someone else sell the remaining stuff so that again you'd be in the clear if anything went wrong. And who would take the word of a Johnny Renaldi—or a Danny Polerri—against that of a respected attorney? But Johnny got wise somehow and grabbed the loose diamonds for himself."

"Why would he do that?"

"Johnny Renaldi," I said, "may not have been smart in your sense of the word, but he knew more about double-crosses than you ever dreamed about. Somewhere along the line you slipped, and he could write the rest of the script blindfolded.

So he grabbed the diamonds and one day he let you know that he had them. I imagine you were a little upset and demanded that he either give them to you or tell you where they were. Renaldi was probably the kind of hood who laughed at you and reminded you that he was the only one who knew where any of the stuff was hidden."

"He had no right to those diamonds," Carleton said. "I told him that I was going to keep them. They had sentimental value for me."

"They have sentimental value for everyone, only it's pronounced 'money.' You'd be surprised how sentimental the insurance company feels about them."

"You've turned them over to the company?"

"No, but I have them where they're safe. And I have not yet finished outlining the case."

"I'm not interested anymore," he said.

"We're coming to the part that interests you the most," I told him. "Obviously, you have some sort of obsession about those diamonds. I think you brooded over the fact that Renaldi had them and wasn't going to return them to you. A few nights ago it became too much for you. You waited until it was late so there wouldn't be much chance of being seen, and then you went to Renaldi's apartment. You took a gun with you because you were going to make him give you the diamonds."

"They were mine," he repeated stubbornly.

"I'd guess that he probably laughed in your face again and then you quarreled. I imagine he made it clear that he wasn't giving up the diamonds, and he may have added that if you kept it up you wouldn't even get to see the other jewelry. And then you shot him."

That produced a moment of silence. Danny Polerri and Mack Larry switched their attention from me to Carleton, who had turned pale with anger.

"You killed Johnny?" Danny Polerri asked in amazement.

"Yes, I did," Carleton said, biting the words crisply. "He was threatening everything we had worked for. He was going to take all of the jewelry for himself. He stood there and laughed and dared me to do anything about it. I had to kill him."

"Sure, you did," I said. "How come you didn't search the apartment after you killed him?"

"I—I was going to, but then I heard someone in the bedroom and I decided I'd better leave before I was seen."

"Thoughtful of you," I murmured.

"Wait a minute," Danny said. He looked at Carleton. "You was going to double-cross us on the diamonds. Johnny was trying to stop that and you shot him. Not the broad. Right?"

"Oh, shut up," Carleton said irritably. "You don't understand all the things that are involved."

"Tell him, Danny," Mack Larry said.

"We both understand," Danny said. "You was trying to cut us out. Maybe Johnny was, too, but it's not the same thing. Maybe you still want to throw us out."

"Of course he does," I said.

"You shut up, too." Carleton said.

"You see," I told Danny, "he doesn't want me to talk either. You think he might be trying to make a sucker out of you?"

"Yeah," Danny said. "What about it, Carleton?"

Carleton's face had turned a dark red. He was again rolling the diamond between his fingers, and then he put it in his pocket. When his hand reappeared, it held a gun. "You're a bunch of scum," he said. "You've been living off of me for months, and you wouldn't have had the chance for this sort of money if it weren't for me."

"Big shot," Danny said scornfully. "Do you think you're going to take both of us?"

Their attention was on each other. I reached down, pulled up the leg of my pants, and took the small gun from the leg holster. I flicked off the safety.

"Or the three of us," I said gently.

It threw all of them off. They turned to look at me and then they saw my gun, and that stopped them for the moment. Carleton had his gun out, but it was pointed in the wrong direction. Danny and Mack had their hands close to their guns, but that was all.

"You're right," I told them. "It's a gun. If you'd like to surrender, I can arrange it."

Carleton reacted first. He said a four-letter word that didn't seem to fit his image and started to swing his gun in my direction. I had plenty of time. I steadied my gun and squeezed the trigger. The bullet hit him in the right shoulder and spun him partly around. His gun dropped from his hand.

I looked at Danny Polerri. He had his gun just clearing his jacket lapel.

"Drop it, Danny," I said.

He was uncertain, and that was his problem. He'd been thinking about shooting Carleton, and now he had to think about me. It was too much, and he couldn't think fast enough, but he was still trying.

I had time, but not enough to be fancy. I shot him through the right leg and he went down, his face twisted in pain. His gun tumbled across the floor.

I switched my gaze to Mack Larry. He had his gun out too, but he saw me look at him and dropped it. It clattered on the floor.

"I cop a plea," he said. "I'm strictly a peterman and I have no ambitions."

"Okay," I said. "Kick your gun over to me—but carefully."

He did as I told him, and the gun slid to within a few inches of my foot.

"Now kick Danny's gun over to me." He obeyed. "Danny has my gun in his pocket. Take it out very slowly and toss it over here."

He reached into Polerri's pocket and brought the gun out, holding it by the barrel, and tossed it over to me. I leaned down and picked it up with my left hand. I switched guns and felt a little better. Small guns always worry me.

"Carleton's gun," I told him. "Kick it over gently. Then go back across the room."

He retreated as soon as the gun slid across the floor. I looked around. Polerri was on the floor, holding his leg, the blood seeping through his fingers. Carleton was sagged back in his chair, his face pale and pinched.

"Take off your coat," I told Mack Larry. When he had it off, I said, "Now your shirt." He obeyed. "Tear it up and tie a strip around Danny's leg. When you've finished that, tie a pad on

Carleton's shoulder. I want to save him for the gas chamber."

While Larry played Dr. Kildare,* I stood up and walked to the phone. I dialed the operator and asked her to get the Beverly Hills police for me. When they answered, I asked for Lieutenant O'Brien. He came on quickly.

"Milo March," I said. "Are you busy?"

"No more than usual," he said acidly. "Did you call to give me some of your well-known cooperation?"

"I had something like that in mind, Lieutenant. I know that it's out of your jurisdiction, but I'm out in Malibu. I have Danny Polerri and Mack Larry with me, as well as an honest citizen of Beverly Hills by the name of Carl Carleton. There are also a few guns, and two of the men are wounded. And there's a confession to murder which was committed in your jurisdiction. Interested?"

He swore. "Where are you?"

I told him and hung up.

O'Brien wasn't long in getting there. Lieutenant Cooper and a state cop were with him. Polerri and Carleton had stopped bleeding, but they weren't talking at the moment. I gave the police the various guns and the tape recording which was in the rear of my car.

"I know you can't use it in court," I told them, "but it might help you in talking to them, and if not you can always keep it as a memento." I went over and retrieved the microphone from the couch. "By the way … you remember the missing diamonds, Lieutenant Cooper?"

---

* The hit TV show *Dr. Kildare* came to an end in August 1966 (about three months before this book was published), but the hero's name became synonymous with the idealized fictional physician.

He nodded. "What about them?"

"You'll find one of them in Carleton's jacket pocket. The one on the right."

He looked in the pocket and came up with the diamond. "Looks like one of them. Where's the rest?"

"I have them. I'll bring them in later."

"Be sure you do."

I watched them load the three men into a car and drive off. I got into the Cadillac and drove wearily back to the city. I parked in front of the apartment and went inside. First I had a drink. Then I took a long shower and changed into fresh clothes. I mixed another drink and sat down to enjoy it. I felt I had earned it. When I finished, I called Kitty Mills.

"Hi, darling," I said when she answered. "How about dinner tonight?"

"Milo!" she said. "How are you?"

"Perfect," I said. "At least, I hope you think so."

"Of course I do, dear."

"You didn't answer the other question."

"Which one?"

"Dinner tonight."

"I'd love it. Sevenish?"

"Aboutish," I answered, and hung up.

There was a paper bag in the kitchen. I emptied the diamonds into it and drove to the Beverly Hills police station. I went in to see Lieutenant Cooper.

"I heard you had a sweet tooth," I told him, putting the bag down on his desk. He turned the bag upside down and the diamonds spilled out over his desk.

"I expect a receipt," I added.

"Pretty baubles," he said. "And you are turning me into a damned accountant. Now, keep quiet for a moment." He counted them carefully, then looked up. "All here but one."

"Carleton's pocket," I said.

He sighed. "Yeah, that's right." He reached for a sheet of paper and wrote out the receipt. "Where did you find these?"

"In Renaldi's second apartment. You should have thought of it."

He swore under his breath. "We searched the joint and didn't find anything."

I gave him my best smile. "Did you look at the water-soaked wallpaper on the ceiling? All you had to do was poke it to make it rain diamonds."

"If there's anything I hate," he said, "it's a smart-assed private eye. You've got your receipt, so get the hell out of here—only be back in time for the trial."

"I wouldn't miss it," I told him, and left.

I made one stop at a phone booth and called Mortimer Harrison. When I got him on the phone, I told him that his client was cleared of the murder charge, but that he might have to represent her on a charge of conspiracy to receive stolen property and at least one charge of burglary. I added that he might get probation for her. I don't think that he appreciated the advice.

Then I went on to Excelsior Mutual. Mr. Hennessey saw me at once. "What can I do for you, Mr. March?" he asked.

"I have," I told him, "a receipt for some jewelry from the Beverly Hills police. Among the gems are the ones insured by your company."

"I know," he said. "I have spoken to the police. I also have a check for you. It is for the sum of eleven thousand, two hundred dollars, which I think you will find correct." He opened a drawer in his desk and produced the check. I took it and examined it with loving care. I was glad to see that it was certified.

"Thanks," I said, putting it away in my pocket.

"I think you're welcome," he said. "Would you tell me one thing, Mr. March? Just between the two of us?"

"Anything, Mr. Hennessey."

"When you came in here with your suggestion—you already knew where the jewelry was, didn't you?"

I stood up. "I couldn't swear to it, but I think that the police already had them. You could check the receipt."

"I'd rather not," he said. "I might have to resign. However, you seem to live up to your reputation and to our agreement, so I don't think our company will have any complaint. Anyway, I think it's been a pleasure doing business with you."

"I can say the same," I said, touching the check in my pocket.

I went downstairs to their bank, which was in the same building. The money felt even better than the check did. Then I drove over to the Intercontinental offices. They had a check for me, too. In fact, they had two checks for me. One covered my per diem fee, and the other was for $10,000 and was my bonus. Both were drawn on a local bank, and I cashed them at once.

I drove back to the apartment, had a drink, and then took a

nap. I was awakened by the phone. It was Martin Raymond calling from New York.

"Mista March not home," I said.

I put the receiver back in its cradle and went in to take a shower. Then I shaved and got dressed, putting the guns away instead of strapping them on. I mixed a martini and sipped it while I telephoned International Airport. I made a reservation for the next morning. I finished the martini and left to pick up Kitty.

We didn't have dinner at the Suckling Pig. We went to Scandia and back to her house right after coffee and brandy. I told her that her jewelry was safe, and then we had a bonus of our own.

The next morning she awakened to look at me. "My goodness," she said, "you're still here. I must have been very special last night."

"You're always very special," I told her. I put out the cigarette I'd been smoking. "The last one in the shower is a sissy."

I beat her to it, which was the way it should be. She was a prettier sissy than I could ever be.

We had waffles for breakfast, with small sausages. I sent her off to get dressed as soon as we'd had coffee. Then I had her get out her Mustang and follow me back to Jed's apartment. The phone was ringing as we entered, but I didn't answer it. I packed my things and again she followed me while I delivered the Cadillac. I tossed my bags in her car and told her to drive me to the airport.

"Are you going back to New York?" she asked.

"No," I said cheerfully, "I'm going on my vacation. Want to come along?"

"Are you serious?"

"Completely."

"Where?"

"It's a secret. We'll get you on the plane and buy you clothes when we get there."

"You're mad," she said. "And I'd love to, but I've got to do that picture."

"Well, that's show biz," I said. "I'll miss you."

"Where are you going?"

I shook my head. "It wouldn't be a vacation if anyone knew. I'll see you on the way back."

We reached the airport and parked. I checked my bags while she went to the cocktail lounge. Then I bought her a drink and firmly sent her off. I had another drink and it was time to board the plane for Hong Kong. As it took off, I thumbed my nose in the general direction of New York.

FOOTNOTES TO A RÉSUMÉ

There are two surviving typewritten résumés of Kendell F. Crossen. The earlier is a xerox copy apparently from 1963. The three-page résumé reproduced here, an undated carbon copy, is likely from 1966, as it lists forthcoming 1967 titles. The following items are notable:

"The Paper Tiger (by Clay Richards)" is listed under Books, page 2, as a forthcoming 1967 publication from Bobbs-Merrill Co. This book was never published. All that remains of the project is a synopsis written by the author. It describes a story in which Kim Locke of the CIA is sent to the Pakistan-India border to foil a plot by Red China.

"Think of Murder" from Green Publishing Co. (Books, page 2): No such title was published. It sounds as if it could be *Murder Out of Mind,* but that was published by Green Publishing in 1945, so you wouldn't expect to be a working title on a 1966 résumé. A mystery!

"Cradle of Crime" (Books, page 2): I at first took this to be a working title for *The Conspiracy of Death,* a nonfiction book about the Mafia in the United States, by George Redston with Kendell Foster Crossen (Bobbs-Merrill, 1965). But since the date given on the résumé is 1967, "Cradle of Crime" may have been a canceled project.

Wanted: Dead Men (Books, page 2) appears on the 1963

KENDELL F. CROSSEN

Credits

NEWSPAPERS

Reporter for the Gallipolis (Ohio) Tribune, the Cleveland (Ohio) Plain Dealer.

Feature writer for the Central Press (Hearst) Syndicate.

Literary critic for the Los Angeles (Calif.) Daily News.

MAGAZINES

Author of 400 published short stories, novelets & articles.

Author of 150 scripts for Superman Comics, Batman Comics, Captain Marvel Comics, Newboy Legion Comics, etc.

Literary critic for Pic and Pageant.

Editor of Detective Fiction Weekly, Baffling Detective Stories, Spark (a picture magazine), Play, Movie Play, Rare Detective Cases and Captain Marvel, Jr. Comics.

Editor & Publisher of Green Lama Comics, Atoman Comics, Golden Boy Comics and Comicland.

BOOKS

Author of the following published books:

THE LAUGHING BUDDHA MURDERS (by Richard Foster) Green Publishing Co.
THE INVISIBLE MAN MURDERS (by Richard Foster) Green Publishing Co.
THE GIRL FROM EASY STREET (by Richard Foster) Popular Books
BLONDE AND BEAUTIFUL (by Richard Foster) Popular Books
THE REST MUST DIE (by Richard Foster) Gold Medal
BIER FOR A CHASER (by Richard Foster) Gold Medal
TOO LATE FOR MOURNING (by Richard Foster) Gold Medal
SATAN COMES ACROSS (By Bennett Barlay) Green Publishing Co.
THE BURNED MAN (by Christopher Monig) E. P. Dutton Co., Inc.
ABRA-CADAVER (by Christopher Monig) E. P. Dutton Co., Inc.
ONCE UPON A CRIME (by Christopher Monig) E. P. Dutton Co., Inc.
THE LONELY GRAVES (by Christopher Monig) E. P. Dutton Co., Inc.
THE MARBLE JUNGLE (by Clay Richards) Ivan Obolensky, Inc.
DEATH OF AN ANGEL (by Clay Richards) The Bobbs-Merrill Co., Inc.

résumé as "Wait for Dead Men," the same title that is on the publisher's contract for this book. It's a little insight into the fact that publishers often demand title changes. *Wanted: Dead Men* actually makes more sense, since classified ads are featured in the plot.

Murder Cavalcade (Books, page 2) was the first of the Mystery Writers of America anthologies, edited by Ken Crossen, whose name is not credited. Most sources give the editor simply as the MWA, but a historical survey on the MWA website (https://mysterywriters.org/about-mwa/mwa-history/) confirms that Crossen was the editor: "To bolster the organization's treasury, MWA set up an anthology series. The first anthology, *Murder Cavalcade,* was published in 1946 by Duell, Sloan, and Pierce. The un-credited editor was Ken Crossen." See also "Mystery Writers Organize Own Murder, Inc.," *New York World-Telegram,* March 26, 1945, p. 14, where the photo caption reads: "The plotters, left to right: Mastermind Baynard Kendrick, president; Moll Marie F. Rodell, secretary; Triggerman Ken Crossen, executive vice president; Dip Clayton Rawson, treasurer."

"Moderator on *Find That Clue* (radio)" is listed under "Radio & Television," page 3. Crossen explained to an interviewer, Steve Lewis, that the show "was on the CBS Pacific Coast network only, and I think it lasted only about six months. I was the moderator, and there were three regular guests and one special guest each week. The regular guests were Craig Rice, Frank Gruber and a radio writer whose name I've forgotten. The special guest was usually an actor or comic. We presented a five-minute (I think) dramatization of a mystery problem, with clues to the solution, and the guests would try to come up with the answers. Everything but the dramatizations was ad-libbed."[*]

Motion Pictures, page 3: *The Man Inside* was made into a

---

[*] "Interview with Kendell Foster Crossen," *The Mystery Nook,* no. 12, June 1979.

WHO STEALS MY NAME (by Clay Richards) The Bobbs-Merrill Co., Inc.
THE GENTLE ASSASSIN (by Clay Richards) The Bobbs-Merrill Co., Inc.
THE PAPER TIGER (by Clay Richards) The Bobbs-Merrill Co., Inc. (1967 Pub.)
THE CASE OF THE CURIOUS HEEL (by Kendell F. Crossen) Green Publishing Co.
THE CASE OF THE PHANTOM FINGERPRINTS (by Kendell F. Crossen) Green
                                     Publishing Co.
THINK OF MURDER (by Kendell F. Crossen) Green Publishing Co.
THE TORTURED PATH (by Kendell F. Crossen) E. P. Dutton Co., Inc.
THE BIG DIVE (by by Kendell F. Crossen) E. P. Dutton Co., Inc.
YEAR OF CONSENT (by Kendell F. Crossen) Dell Publishing Co.
ONCE UPON A STAR (by Kendell F. Crossen) Henry Holt, Inc.
COMEBACK ([non-fiction] by Kendell F. Crossen) The Bobbs-Merrill Co., Inc.
THE CONSPIRACY OF DEATH ([non-fiction] by Kendell F. Crossen) The
                                   Bobbs-Merrill Co., Inc.
CRADLE OF CRIME ([non-fiction] by Kendell F. Crossen) The Bobbs-Merrill
                                   Co., Inc. (1967 Pub.)
HANGMAN'S HARVEST (by M. E. Chaber) Henry Holt, Inc.
NO GRAVE FOR MARCH (by M. E. Chaber) Henry Holt, Inc.
THE MAN INSIDE (by M. E. Chaber) Henry Holt, Inc.
AS OLD AS CAIN (by M. E. Chaber) Henry Holt, Inc.
THE SPLINTERED MAN (by M. E. Chaber) Rinehart, Inc.
A LONELY WALK (by M. E. Chaber) Rinehart, Inc.
THE GALLOWS GARDEN (by M. E. Chaber) Rinehart, Inc.
A HEARSE OF ANOTHER COLOR (by M. E. Chaber) Rinehart, Inc.
SO DEAD THE ROSE (by M. E. Chaber) Rinehart, Inc.
JADE FOR A LADY (by M. E. Chaber) Holt, Rinehart & Winston, Inc.
SOFTLY IN THE NIGHT (by M. E. Chaber) Holt, Rinehart & Winston, Inc.
UNEASY LIES THE DEAD (by M. E. Chaber) Holt, Rinehart & Winston, Inc.
SIX WHO RAN (by M. E. Chaber) Holt, Rinehart & Winston, Inc.
WANTED: DEAD MEN (by M. E. Chaber) Holt, Rinehart & Winston, Inc.
THE DAY IT RAINED DIAMONDS (by M. E. Chaber) Holt, Rinehart & Winston,
                                   Inc. (Nov. 1966)
THE MAN IN THE MIDDLE (M. E. Chaber) Holt, Rinehart & Winston, Inc.
                                   (out in 1967)
THE ACID NIGHTMARE (by M. E. Chaber) Holt, Rinehart & Winston, Inc.
                                   (out in 1967)

Editor of the following anthologies:

MURDER CAVALCADE (Kendell F. Crossen) Duell, Sloane & Pearce, Inc.
ADVENTURES IN TOMORROW (Kendell F. Crossen) Greenberg: Publisher
FUTURE TENSE (Kendell F. Crossen) Greenberg: Publisher

Special consulting editor for Simon & Schuster, Henry Holt, Inc., Duell,
Sloane & Pearce, Inc. and Greenberg: Publisher.

RADIO & TELEVISION

Kate Smith Show (radio)
Ed Wynn Show (radio)
Stoopnagel & Bud (radio)
The Arkansas Traveler (radio)
Molle Mystery Theatre (radio)
The Saint (radio)

film directed by John Gilling, released in September 1958 in the UK (December in the US). Credit for the screenplay went to David Shaw and John Gilling; Ken Crossen's name was not mentioned. *The Rest Must Die* (a science fiction novel) and *The Splintered Man* were not made into movies. I don't know

The Green Lama (radio)
Major North (radio)
Adventure (radio)
Sam Spade (radio)
Suspense (radio)

Director of The Falcon (radio)
Editor & rewrite man for Suspense (radio)
Special Consulting Editor (radio - NBC)
Special Consulting Editor (radio -CBS)
Moderator on Find That Clue (radio)

Perry Mason (TV)
Man & The Challenge (TV)
Collectors Item (TV)
The Man From Blackhawk (TV)
Plus many pilot scripts for CBS and for Harry Ackerman at Screen Gems

MOTION PICTURES

Untitled original for King Brothers (in collaboration with Paul Francis
                                                              Webster)
The Man Inside - Original story for Columbia-Warwick
The Rest Must Die - Original story for a N.Y. independent
The Splintered Man - Original story for Pinetree Productions

what the untitled project for King Brothers in collaboration with Paul Francis Webster could have been. Another mystery.

An earlier résumé (1963) says that Crossen wrote the screenplay for the motion picture *"Panic* (original story)," directed by Gilling. The storyline, about a gang planning a diamond heist, does sound very much like one of Ken's pulp plots. But online, Guido Coen and John Gilling are credited for the screenplay of the 1963 film, and *Panic* does not appear on this later résumé.

Kendra Crossen Burroughs

Mystery Writers Organize Own Murder Inc.

Assassination Club Set Up in Times Sq., In Broad Daylight

By THOMAS COPE,
World-Telegram Staff Writer.

A dark deed was done at the crossroads of America today. A small, distinguished band of experts in murder gumshoed into a dingy office near Times Sq. A silken-voiced young woman with beautiful, deadly eyes fished a legal document out of a wastebasket with a false bottom.

The assembled experts gloated over the vellum, which set forth articles of incorporation under the laws of the State of New York. Then with lethal grins they elected officers pro-tem, and disbanded, each in search of a bottle of Scotch for the first annual party, to take place somewhere, somehow, next month.

All Done with Pens.

Thus was born Mystery Writers of America, Inc., whose stated aim is to provide a clearing house of technical information and other tools of the trade for the men and women—many with families, and respected by their neighbors—whose lucrative business it is to assassinate fellow-humans (and sometimes the King's English) on paper.

Though ostensibly a static, intramural cell, MWA, Inc., is in reality a merciless pressure group patterned after the infamous Detection Club of London, of which the late beloved G. K. Chesterton was the first president and whose surviving members—Dorothy Sayers, John Dickson Carr, etc.—were described in blood-chilling prose by Anthony Berkely in "The Case of the Poison Chocolates."

"Sure we want publicity," hoarsely whispered the Mastermind (president) Baynard Kendrick, creator of the blind detective, Duncan Maclain. "Only four people out of five read detective stories, which they have borrowed from the fifth person, who probably stole the book from a library."

Anthology of Crime.

The other officers of MWA are Triggerman (executive vice president) Ken Crossen ("The Case of the Curious Heel"), former editor of Detective Fiction Weekly; Dip (treasurer) Clayton Rawson, editor of True Detective, and Moll or No-Girl (secretary) Marie F. Rodell—the most sinister and beautiful character of them all, being the author of "Mystery Fiction: Theory and Technique," and other snake books.

The board of directors includes a dozen names such as Mignon G. Eberhart, Anthony Boucher, Ellery Queen, Mabel Seeley. Membership, by invitation, will come from the ranks of about 200 whodunit book authors and an indeterminate number of magazine and radio mystery writers.

The club will edit an anthology, award annual prizes for the best mystery novel, radio serial and movie, and occasionally, it is hoped, hear lectures by such authorities as Edgar J. Hoover, Police Commissioner Valentine and Chief Inspector John J. O'Connor.

"But first," said Mastermind Kendrick, "we've got to find clubrooms. Anybody want to rent out a warehouse basement?"

The plotters, left to right: Mastermind Baynard Kendrick, president; Moll Marie F. Rodell, secretary; Triggerman Ken Crossen, executive vice president; Dip Clayton Rawson, treasurer.

World-Telegram Photo by Aumuller.

ABOUT THE AUTHOR

Kendell Foster Crossen
(1910–1981), the only child
of Samuel Richard Cros-
sen and Clo Foster Cros-
sen, was born on a farm
outside Albany in Athens
County, Ohio—a village of
some 550 souls in the year
of this birth. His ancestors
on his mother's side include
the 19th-century songwriter
Stephen Collins Foster
("Oh! Susanna"); William
Allen, founder of Allentown, Pennsylvania; and Ebenezer
Foster, one of the Minute Men who sprang to arms at the
Lexington alarm in April 1775.

Ken went to Rio Grande College on a football scholarship
but stayed only one year. "When I was fairly young, I devel-
oped the disgusting habit of reading," says Milo March,
and it seems Ken Crossen, too, preferred self-education.
He loved literature and poetry; favorite authors included
Christopher Marlowe and Robert Service. He also enjoyed
participant sports and was a semi-pro fighter in the heavy-

weight class. He became a practicing magician and had a passion for chess.

After college Ken wrote several one-act plays that were produced in a small Cleveland theater. He worked in steel mills and Fisher Body plants. Then he was employed as an insurance investigator, or "claims adjuster," in Cleveland. But he left the job and returned to the theater, now as a performer: a tumbling clown in the Tom Mix Circus; a comic and carnival barker for a tent show, and an actor in a medicine show.

In 1935, Ken hitchhiked to New York City with a typewriter under his arm, and found work with the WPA Writers' Project, covering cricket for the *New York City Guidebook*. In 1936, he was hired by the Munsey Publishing Company as associate editor of the popular *Detective Fiction Weekly*. The company asked him to come up with a character to compete with The Shadow, and thus was born a unique superhero of pulps, comic books, and radio—The Green Lama, an American mystic trained in Tibetan Buddhism.

Crossen sold his first story, "The Aaron Burr Murder Case," to *Detective Fiction Weekly* in September 1939, but says he didn't begin to make a living from writing till 1941. He tried his hand at publishing true crime magazines, comics, and a picture magazine, without great success, so he set out for Hollywood. From his typewriter flowed hundreds of stories, short novels for magazines, scripts radio, television, and film, nonfiction articles. He delved into science fiction in the 1950s, starting with "Restricted Clientele" (February 1951). His dystopian novels *Year of Consent* and *The Rest Must Die* also appeared in this decade.

In the course of his career Ken Crossen acquired six pseud-
onyms: Richard Foster, Bennett Barlay, Kent Richards, Clay
Richards, Christopher Monig, and M.E. Chaber. The variety
was necessary because different publishers wanted to reserve
specific bylines for their own publications. Ken based "M.E.
Chaber" on the Hebrew word for "author," *mechaber.*

In the early '50s, as M.E. Chaber, Crossen began to write
a series of full-length mystery/espionage novels featuring
Milo March, an insurance investigator. The first, *Hangman's
Harvest,* was published in 1952. In all, there are twenty-two
Milo March novels. One, *The Man Inside,* was made into a
British film starring Jack Palance.

Most of Ken's characters were private detectives, and Milo
was the most popular. Paperback Library reissued twenty-five
Crossen titles in 1970–1971, with covers by Robert McGinnis. Twenty were Milo March novels, four featured an insurance investigator named Brian Brett, and one was about CIA
agent Kim Locke.

Crossen excelled at producing well-plotted entertainment
with fast-moving action. His research skills were a strong
asset, back when research meant long hours searching library
microfilms and poring over street maps and hotel floorplans.
His imagination took him to many international hot spots,
although he himself never traveled abroad. Like Milo March,
he hated flying ("When you've seen one cloud, you've seen
them all").

Ken Crossen was married four times. With his first wife he
had three children (Stephen, Karen, Kendra) and with his
second a son (David). He lived in New York, Florida, South-

ern California, Nevada, and other parts of the country. Milo March moves from Denver to New York City after five books of the series, with an apartment on Perry Street in Greenwich Village; that's where Ken lived, too. His and Milo's favorite watering hole was the Blue Mill Tavern, a short walk from the apartment.

Ken Crossen was a combination of many of the traits of his different male characters: tough, adventuresome, with a taste for gin and shapely women. But perhaps the best observation was made in an obituary written by sci-fi writer Avram Davidson, who described Ken as a fundamentally gentle person who had been buffeted by many winds.

Made in the USA
Middletown, DE
07 November 2020